T0027164

75
FSG

TOVE DITLEVSEN

Dependency

Tove Ditlevsen was born in 1917 in a working-class neighborhood in Copenhagen. Her first volume of poetry was published when she was in her early twenties and was followed by many more books, including the three volumes of the Copenhagen Trilogy: *Childhood* (1967), *Youth* (1967), and *Dependency* (1971). She died in 1976.

BY TOVE DITLEVSEN

THE COPENHAGEN TRILOGY

Book 1: Childhood

Book 2: Youth

Book 3: Dependency

Dependency

Dependency

THE COPENHAGEN TRILOGY: BOOK 3

TOVE DITLEVSEN

Translated from the Danish by
MICHAEL FAVALA GOLDMAN

FSG ORIGINALS | FARRAR, STRAUS AND GIROUX | NEW YORK

FSG Originals
Farrar, Straus and Giroux
120 Broadway, New York 10271

Copyright © 1971 by Tove Ditlevsen & Gyldendal, Copenhagen
Translation copyright © 2019 by Michael Favala Goldman
All rights reserved
Printed in the United States of America
Originally published in Danish in 1971 in Denmark as *Gift*
English translation first published in 2019 by Penguin Random House, Great Britain
Published in the United States by Farrar, Straus and Giroux
First American edition, 2021

Library of Congress Cataloging-in-Publication Data
Names: Ditlevsen, Tove Irma Margit, 1917–1976, author. | Goldman, Michael (Michael Favala), translator.
Title: Dependency / Tove Ditlevsen ; translated from the Danish by Michael Favala Goldman.
Other titles: Gift. English
Description: First American edition. | New York : Farrar, Straus and Giroux, 2021. | Series: The Copenhagen trilogy; book 3 | "Originally published in Danish in 1971 in Denmark as Gift"
Identifiers: LCCN 2020035111 | ISBN 9780374539412 (paperback)
Subjects: LCSH: Ditlevsen, Tove Irma Margit, 1917–1976. | Authors, Danish—20th century—Biography.
Classification: LCC PT8175.D5 Z46 2021d | DDC 839.813/72 [B]—dc23
LC record available at https://lccn.loc.gov/2020035111

Our books may be purchased in bulk for promotional, educational, or business use. Please contact your local bookseller or the Macmillan Corporate and Premium Sales Department at 1-800-221-7945, extension 5442, or by e-mail at MacmillanSpecialMarkets@macmillan.com.

www.fsgbooks.com • www.fsgoriginals.com
Follow us on Twitter, Facebook, and Instagram at @fsgoriginals

10 9 8 7 6 5 4 3 2 1

PART ONE

I

Everything in the living room is green – the carpet, the walls, the curtains – and I am always inside it, like in a picture. I wake up every morning around five o'clock and sit down on the edge of the bed to write, curling my toes because of the cold. It's the middle of May, and the heating is off. I sleep by myself in the living room, because Viggo F. has lived alone for so many years that he can't get used to suddenly sleeping with another person. I understand, and it's fine with me, because now I have these early morning hours all to myself. I'm writing my first novel, and Viggo F. doesn't know. Somehow I think that if he knew, he would correct it and give me advice, like he does all the other young people who write in *Wild Wheat*, and then that would block the flow of sentences coursing through my brain all day long. I write by hand on cheap yellow vellum, because if I used his noisy typewriter, which is so old it belongs in the National Museum, it would wake him up. He sleeps in the bedroom looking out on the courtyard, and I don't wake him until eight o'clock. Then he gets up in his white nightshirt with the red trim, and with an annoyed look on his face, he walks out to the bathroom.

Meanwhile I make coffee for both of us and butter four pieces of bread. I put a lot of butter on two of them, because he loves anything fattening. I do whatever I can to please him, because I'm so thankful he married me. Although I know something still isn't quite right, I carefully avoid thinking about that. For some incomprehensible reason, Viggo F. has never taken me in his arms, and that does bother me a little, as if I had a stone in my shoe. It bothers me a little because I think there must be something wrong with me, and that in some way I haven't lived up to his expectations. When we sit across from one another, drinking coffee, he reads the newspaper, and I'm not allowed to talk to him. That's when my courage drains away like sand in an hourglass; I don't know why. I stare at his double chin, vibrating weakly, spilling out over the edge of his wing-tip collar. I stare at his small, dainty hands, moving in short, nervous jerks, and at his thick, gray hair which resembles a wig, because his ruddy, wrinkle-free face would better suit a bald man. When we finally do talk to one another, it's about small, meaningless things – what he wants for dinner, or how we should fix the tear in the blackout curtains. I feel glad if he finds something cheerful in the newspaper, like the day when it said people could buy alcohol again, after the occupying forces had forbidden that for a week. I feel glad when he smiles at me with his single tooth, pats my hand, says goodbye and leaves. He doesn't want false teeth, because he says that in his family men die at fifty-six, and that's only three years away, so he doesn't want the expense. There's no hiding the fact that he's stingy, and that doesn't really match the high value my mother put on being able to provide. He's never given me a piece of clothing, and when we go out in the evening to visit some famous person, he takes the streetcar, while I have to ride my bicycle alongside it, speeding along so I can wave to him when he wants. I have to keep a household budget, and when he looks at it, he always thinks everything is too expensive. When I can't get it to add up, I write 'miscellaneous', but he always makes a fuss about that, so I try not to miss any expenses. He also makes a fuss about having a housekeeper in the mornings, since I'm home anyway, doing nothing. But I can't and won't keep house, so he has no choice. I feel glad when I see him cut across the green lawn toward the streetcar, which stops right in front of the police station. I wave to him, and when I turn away from the window, I completely forget about him until he shows up again. I take a shower, look in the mirror, and think to myself that I am only twenty years old, and that it feels like I have been married for a generation. It feels like life beyond these green rooms is rushing by for other people as if to the sound of kettledrums and tom-toms. Meanwhile I am only twenty years old, and the days descend on me unnoticeably like dust, each one just like the rest.

After I get dressed, I talk with Mrs Jensen about lunch and I make a list of what needs to be purchased. Mrs Jensen is taciturn, introverted and a bit insulted that she's not alone in the house anymore, like she used to be. What nonsense, she mumbles, that a man of his age would marry such a young girl. She doesn't say it so loud that I have to answer, and I can't be bothered to listen to what she says. I'm thinking about my novel all the time, which I know the title of, though I'm not completely sure what it will be about. I'm just writing; maybe it will be good; maybe not. The most important thing is that I feel happy when I'm writing, just as I always have. I feel happy and I forget everything around me, until I pick up my brown shoulder bag and go shopping. Then I'm gripped again by the morning's vague gloom, because all I see in the streets are loving couples walking hand in hand and looking deep into one another's eyes. I almost can't bear the sight of it. I realize I've never been in love, except for a brief episode two years before, when I walked home from the Olympia Bar with Kurt, who was going to be leaving the following day for Spain to take part in the civil war. He might be dead now, or maybe he came back and found himself another girl. Maybe I didn't really have to marry Viggo F. to make it in the world. Maybe I only did it because my mother wanted me to so badly. I poke a finger into the meat to see if it feels tender. This is something my mother has taught me. And I write on my little notepaper what it costs, because I'll forget before I get home. When the shopping is done and Mrs Jensen has left, I put everything out of my mind so I can hammer away at the typewriter, now that it won't disturb anyone.

My mother comes and visits me regularly, and together we can be pretty silly. A couple of days after I got married, she opened up the closet and looked through Viggo F.'s clothes. She calls him 'Viggomand', because she has just as much trouble as other people calling him by his real name. I can't do it either, because there is something immature about the name Viggo when it's not referring to a child. She held all his green clothing up to the light and found a set that was so moth-eaten, she thought it couldn't be worn anymore. Mrs Brun could use this to sew me a dress, she concluded. It was never any use to oppose my mother when she made a decision like that, so offering no resistance, I let her leave with the clothes, hoping that Viggo F. wouldn't ask about it. Sometime later we visited my parents. We don't do that very often, because there's something about the way Viggo F. talks to them that I can't stand. He speaks loudly and slowly, as if to mentally disabled children, and he searches carefully for subjects he thinks might interest them. We visited them, and suddenly he prodded me with a confidential elbow in my side. What a coincidence, he said, twirling his mustache between his thumb and forefinger. Did you notice that the fabric of your mother's dress exactly matches a set of clothes I have hanging in the closet at home? Then my mother and I dashed from the room and burst out laughing.

During this period I feel very close to my mother, and I'm not harboring any deep and painful feelings about her anymore. She is two years younger than her son-in-law, and they never talk about anything except how I was as a child. I don't recognize myself at all in my mother's early impressions of me; it's like they're talking about a different child altogether. When my mother comes to visit, I stuff my novel away in my locked drawer in Viggo F.'s desk. I make coffee and we drink it while we chat. We talk about how good it is that my father has gotten steady work at the Ørsted factory, about Edvin's cough, and about all the alarming symptoms from my mother's internal organs, which have plagued her ever since Aunt Rosalia's death. I think my mother is still pretty and youthful. She's petite and her face is nearly wrinkle-free, just like Viggo F.'s. Her permed hair is thick as a doll's, and she always sits on the edge of her chair, with a straight back and her hands on the handles of her purse. She sits the same way Aunt Rosalia always did when she only was going to stay 'a brief moment', and then didn't leave until several hours had passed. My mother leaves before Viggo F. comes home from the fire insurance company, because he is usually in a bad mood then and doesn't like it if anyone is here. He hates his work at the office and he hates the people there, too. He has something against everyone, I think, unless they happen to be artists.

After we've eaten and gone over the household budget, he

usually asks how far I've come with *The French Revolution*, which is supposed to be part of my basic education, so I make sure that I have read at least a few new pages in it. After I've carried out the dishes, he lies down to rest on the divan, and I glance at the blue globe outside the police station, which illuminates the deserted courtyard with a glassy light. Then I roll down the shades, sit down and read Carlyle until Viggo F. wakes up and wants coffee. While we drink it, and if we don't have to go out to visit some famous person, a strange silence spreads between us. It's as if everything we might have said to one another was used up before we were married, as if we spent all the words that ought to have lasted the next twenty-five years; because I don't believe he's going to die in three years. The only thing occupying my thoughts is my novel, and since I can't talk about that, I don't know what to talk about. A month ago, just after the occupation started, Viggo F. was alarmed because he thought the Germans were going to arrest him, since he had written an article in the *Social-Demokraten* about the concentration camps. So we talked about what might happen. And in the evening his equally frightened friends, who had similarly troubled consciences, came by. But now they all seem to have forgotten about the danger, and they live mostly as if nothing ever happened. Every day I'm afraid that he will ask me if I have finished reading his manuscript for the new novel he'll be sending to Gyldendal Publishing. It's lying on his desk, and I've tried to read it, but it's so boring and wordy and full of knotty, incorrect sentences, that I don't think I will ever be able to get through it. That also makes the atmosphere between us tense – that I don't like his books. I've never said that out loud, but I've never praised them either. I've just said that I don't understand much about literature.

Though our evenings at home are sad and uniform, I still prefer them to the evenings with the famous artists. When I am with them I'm gripped by shyness and awkwardness, and it's as if my mouth were full of sawdust, because it's impossible for me to come up with clever answers to their jovial remarks. They talk about their paintings, their exhibitions or about their books, and they read aloud poems they have just written. For me, writing is like it was in my childhood, something secret and prohibited, shameful, something one sneaks into a corner to do when no one else is watching. They ask me what I am writing at the moment, and I say, Nothing. Viggo F. comes to my rescue. She's reading right now, he says. You have to read an awful lot to be able to write prose, and that will be the next thing. He talks about me almost as if I weren't present, and I'm relieved when we finally get up to go. When he's with famous people, Viggo F. is a completely different person – cheerful, self-confident, witty – just like he was with me in the beginning.

One evening, out at the home of the illustrator Arne Ungermann, they mentioned wanting to gather together all the young people who are published in *Wild Wheat*, since they are most likely very lonely, scattered around Copenhagen. They would probably be happy to get to know one another. Then Tove could be the head of the association, says Viggo F., giving me a friendly smile. Thinking about that makes me happy, since otherwise I only see young people when they venture out to us with their work, and they barely even glance at me then, since I'm married to this important man. My elation frees up my tongue and I say it could be called 'The Young Artists Club'. The idea draws general applause.

The next day I find the addresses in Viggo F.'s notebook, and in a few brief phrases I write a very formal letter in which

I suggest a meeting at our home one particular evening in the near future. Then I deposit all the letters in the mailbox beside the police station, imagining how happy they will be, because I think that they're poor and lonely like I was not long ago, and that they're sitting in ice-cold, rented rooms all around the city. It occurs to me that Viggo F. knows me quite well after all. He knows I'm tired of only being around old people. He knows that I often feel suffocated by life in his green rooms, and that I can't spend my entire youth reading about the French Revolution.

2

The Young Artists Club is now a reality and my life has regained color and substance. Every Thursday evening about a dozen of us meet, in a room in the Women's Building that we got permission to use as long as we each buy a cup of coffee. It costs one krone per person, without cake, and those who don't have money borrow it from those who do. The meeting starts with a lecture by a famous older artist – a 'Big Fish' – who thereby does Viggo F. a friendly favor. I never hear a word of the lecture, because I'm too preoccupied with having to stand up and thank them when it's over. I always say the same thing: Let me thank you for that excellent lecture. It was very kind of you to come. Usually, to our relief, the Big Fish declines our offer to stay for coffee. Then the rest of us pass the time, chatting cheerfully about everything under the sun, but rarely naming who brought us together. At the most, one of them might say to me incidentally, Do you happen to know if Møller liked the two poems I sent him recently? They all call him Møller and speak of him with veneration. Thanks to him they're not unknowns; thanks to him, if they're lucky, once in a while they'll get to see their names in a review of *Wild Wheat*, which has always enjoyed attention from the media. There are only three girls in the club – Sonja Hauberg, Ester Nagel and myself. The two of them are pretty, serious, dark-haired, dark-eyed and from wealthy homes. Sonja studied literature, and Ester works in a pharmacy. All of us are about twenty years old except for Piet Hein, who is the only one who doesn't seem to respect Viggo F. very much. Piet Hein makes a fuss over the fact I have to be home by eleven, and that I can never go with him afterwards to the Hungarian Vinhus. But I always arrive home on time, because Viggo F. is sitting up, waiting for me, to hear how the evening went. He waits there with coffee or a glass of wine, and at those times I see him through my friends' eyes. This usually makes me want to show him my half novel, but in the end I can't bring myself to do it. Piet Hein has a face as round as a pie, and a sharp tongue, which frightens me a bit. When he walks me home at night through the blacked-out moonlit city, he stops at the canal or in front of the stock-exchange building with its green copper luminous roof, opens my hands like a book, and kisses me long and deep. He asks me why I married that troglodyte, when I'm so beautiful I could have almost anyone I choose. I answer obliquely, because I don't like it when anyone makes fun of Viggo F. I don't think Piet Hein knows what it's like to have been poor and to have had to use nearly every second of your life just to survive. I have more compassion for Halfdan Rasmussen, who is short, skinny, badly dressed, and living off public support. He and I had the same kind of upbringing and we speak the same language. But Halfdan is in love with Ester, Morten Nielsen with Sonja, and Piet Hein with me. We figured this out within a few Thursdays. I'm not sure if I'm in love with Piet Hein. When he kisses me I get aroused, but he also confuses me when he wants me to do a ton of things all at once, like: marry him, have children, and meet a girl he knows because he thinks I need a girlfriend. When Piet takes me in his arms, he calls me 'Kitten'.

One evening he brings the girl to the club. Her name is Nadja and she is obviously in love with him. She is taller than me, thin, slightly stooped and with an uneven, sloppy expression on her face, as if she lives too much for other people, so she never has time for herself. I really like her. She works at a garden center and she lives with her father, who is Russian and divorced. She invites me over, and I go to visit, after telling Viggo F. about her. Their apartment is large and grand, and Nadja entertains me with stories about Piet Hein while we drink tea. She says that he likes to have two girlfriends at once. When she first got to know him he was married, and he made sure that she became friends with his wife before he left her. But they aren't friends anymore. It's just something he cooked up, says Nadja calmly. She asks me about my life and suggests I get divorced from Viggo F. That idea had also just occurred to me. I tell her about our nonexistent sex life, and she says it's a sin and a shame that he has doomed me to childlessness. You should get advice about it from Piet, she says. As long as he's hot for you, he'll do anything you ask.

So I do that, one evening while we're standing quietly by the canal, the water sloshing against the wharf with a soft, lazy sound. I ask Piet how a person gets divorced, and he says that he'll take care of all the practical matters. All I have to do is tell my husband. Piet says he'll pay for me to live in a boarding house, and that he'll take better care of me than Viggo F. does. I say, I might be able to support myself; I'm writing a novel. I say this matter-of-factly, as if I have written twenty novels and this is just number twenty-one. Piet asks me if he can read it, and I say no one can read it until it's finished. Then he asks if he could invite me over to his place for dinner one night. He lives on Store Kongensgade in a little apartment, where he set himself up when he got divorced. I say yes, and then I tell Viggo F. that I'm going out to visit my parents. It's the first time I've lied to him, and I feel ashamed when he believes me. Viggo F. is sitting at his desk, laying out *Wild Wheat*. He's cutting out drawings, stories and poems from the proofs, then gluing them into the pages of an old issue. He does this so delicately, and his whole body, with the big head bent beneath the green lamp, radiates something resembling happiness, because he loves that journal the way other people love their families. I kiss him on his soft, damp mouth and suddenly I get tears in my eyes. We have something together – not much, but something – and now I am starting to destroy it. I'm sad that my life is about to get complicated as never before. But I also think how strange it is that I never go against what anyone else wants; not really. I might be home a bit late, I say. My mother isn't feeling well. So don't wait up.

Well, says Piet jovially, wasn't that good?

Yes, I say, happily. Since my affair with Aksel I've been wondering if maybe there was something wrong with me in that department, but there isn't. Piet and I have had food and drink, and I'm a bit tipsy. We're lying in a wide canopy bed that Piet got from his mother, who is an eye doctor. The room is furnished with funny lamps, modern furniture and a polar-bear skin on the floor. In a vase by the bed there's a rose which is already starting to lose its petals. Piet gave it to me. He has given me a blue flannel dress too, which has to hang at his place for the time being. I can't just take it home. I pick up the rose and sniff it. It doesn't want to just be grafted anymore, I laugh. I can use that, exclaims Piet, jumping out of bed completely naked. He sits down at his desk, grabs a pen and paper and scribbles something down. When he's done he shows it to me. It's a grook for the *Politiken* newspaper, for whom he writes these four-line witty stanzas every day. It reads:

> I placed a rose by my lover's bed
> It blushed, sweet aroma wafting
> First one petal fell then two and more
> Now it doesn't believe in grafting.

I praise him for it, and he says that I should get half the honorarium. For Piet, being a writer is not something to hide or be ashamed of. To him it is as straightforward as breathing.

This is going to be a tough pill for Møller to swallow, he says with satisfaction. When you got married, all his friends bet on how long it would last – more than one year or less. No one thought it would last longer than one year. And then Robert Mikkelsen provided the pre-nuptial agreement, because they all thought you would take half his property.

I'm shocked. I say, You are so wicked. And conniving.

No, says Piet, it's just I don't like him. He's a parasite of the arts without being an artist himself. He can't even write.

Feeling ill at ease I say, That's not his fault. And I don't like it when you talk about him like that; it puts me in a bad mood. I ask what time it is, and my brief happiness slips away. A wet, silvery stillness fills the room, as if something fateful is about to happen. I don't hear what Piet says. I'm thinking about Viggo F., bent beneath his desk lamp, laying out his journal. I'm thinking about the bet his friends made and about the impossibility of saying to him that we have to split up. Sometimes, Piet says tenderly, you get very distant, and I can't reach you. You are so fascinating and I think I'm in love with you. Can I write to you? He asks, Does the mail arrive after he leaves? Yes, I say, you can write to me. The next day I get a love letter from Piet: Dear Kitten, You are the only girl I could ever imagine marrying. I get anxious and I telephone Viggo F. What is it? he asks, a bit shortly. I don't know, I say. I just feel very alone. All right, he says. I'll be home tonight, okay?

Then I take out my novel and I write and write and forget about everything. The novel is nearly finished. The title is going to be *A Child Was Harmed*. In one way or another it's about me, even though I may never experience the things the people do in the book.

3

And this, says Viggo F., twirling his mustache, a sign that he is in a good mood – have you hidden this from me all this time? He's sitting with my manuscript in his hand, looking up at me with his bright blue eyes, which are so clear it's like they've just been washed. Everything about him is clean and dapper, and he gives off the scent of soap and shaving lotion. His breath is fresh as a baby's, because he doesn't smoke.

Yes, I say, I wanted to surprise you. Do you really think it's good?

It's stunning, he says. There's not a comma out of place. This will be a huge success.

I can tell I'm blushing with happiness. In that moment I couldn't care less about Piet Hein or my divorce plans. Once more Viggo F. is the person I have dreamed of meeting my entire life. He pulls out a bottle of wine and pours it into the green glasses. Cheers, he says, smiling. And congratulations. We agree again to try Gyldendal first, even though they didn't want my poems. They have recently accepted the novel by Viggo F. that I couldn't get through. He just said that I was too young to have a feel for his writing, and that it couldn't be helped. This one evening we enjoy each other's company as it was before we were married, and the thought of what I will soon say to him seems distant and unreal, like the thought of what could happen in ten years. That was the last evening we were really close. We were alone together behind the black-out curtains in the green living room, sharing something the world had not yet seen, and we talked about my first novel until it was past our bedtime, and we both yawned between drinks of wine. Viggo F. never gets drunk, and he can't stand when other people do. He threw out Johannes Weltzer many times, when, tipsy, enthusiastic and sweating, he paced our floor while talking about the novel he was writing. He'll talk it to death, says Viggo F., who thinks Johannes has only written one good sentence in his whole life. It was: 'Dear to me are restlessness and long trips.' The expectation that one should drink in moderation, similar to the expectation that one should leave at the appropriate time, is always hanging in the air. We have company quite often. At those times I go shopping in a delicatessen on Amagerbrogade, because like my mother, I hardly know how to prepare food other than the most basic things.

One day I tell my mother I'm planning to get divorced. I tell her about Piet Hein, about all the gifts he has given me, and about how he is going to take care of my future. My mother wrinkles her brow and thinks for a long time. On the street where I grew up no one ever got divorced. The couples there might argue and fight like cats and dogs, but they never mention divorce. That must be something that only happens among higher society; no one knows why.

But will he marry you? she asks finally, rubbing her nose with her index finger, as she always does when something is troubling her. I say that he hasn't talked about it, but that he probably will. I say that I can't bear staying married to Viggo F., and that every day I feel heartsick when it's time for him to come home. I say that the marriage has been a mistake for both of us. Yes, she says, I understand, in a way. It does look rather dumb when you two walk down the street, since he's so much shorter than you. My mother lacks the ability to put herself in other people's shoes, which keeps her from hurting my feelings, and that suits me fine.

Now I go home with Piet Hein every Thursday after the meeting. I tell Viggo F. that the discussions after the lecture last so long, and that as chairperson it wouldn't be proper if I were the first to leave. I tell him not to wait up for me, but to just go to bed. When he's asleep, nothing can wake him up, and he doesn't know how late I come home. But why, says Piet impatiently, why don't you tell him? I keep promising to tell Viggo F. the next day, but in the end I doubt that I will ever be able to get the words out. I'm afraid how he will react. I'm afraid of arguing and scenes, and I always think with horror about when my father and brother fought every night, so there was never any peace in our little living room. If you can't tell him, says Piet one evening, you can just move out, just like that. You can't take anything but your clothes with you anyway. But I can't do it. It would be too mean, too brutal, too ungrateful. Piet also asks me to pay more attention to Nadja, who is miserable because he left her. I visit her frequently. She sits in a metal chair, stretching out her long legs and rubbing her face irritably, as if she wanted to rearrange her features. She says that Piet is dangerous, created to make women unhappy. Now that he has left her, she's going to change her life. She's going to attend the university and study psychology, because she has always been more interested in other people than in herself. And that will save her. She says sadly, He'll leave you, too. One day he'll come to you and say, I've found someone else. But I'm sure you'll take it on the chin. Take it on the chin is his favorite expression. She also says that I'm going to get divorced anyway, and that Piet is as good an excuse as anyone. I don't pay too much attention to what she says, because when it comes down to it, she's bitter about being deserted.

Sometimes Piet Hein bothers me, like when I'm lying with his arm around me, and he's conjuring up plans for my future. It bothers me that he wants to rummage in my life and arrange it, as if I were unable to take care of it myself, and I wish he would just leave me alone. I wish I could move back and forth between him and Viggo F. without losing either of them and with no radical upheavals. I've always avoided change and been comforted by things staying the way they are. But it can't go on. Now I'm able to look at loving couples in the street again, but I turn away from the sight of mothers with small children. I avoid looking in baby carriages or thinking about the girls from my old street, who were so proud that they waited until they were eighteen to have children. I suppress all those kinds of thoughts because Piet is careful not to get me pregnant. He says that women authors shouldn't have children; there are plenty of other women who can. On the other hand, there aren't so many who can write books.

My misery gets dramatically worse toward five o'clock in the afternoon. While I'm standing in the kitchen turning on the potatoes, my heart starts hammering and the white tile wall behind the stovetop flickers before my eyes, as if the tiles were starting to fall off. When Viggo F. walks in the door with his dark, irritated face, I start talking feverishly as if to defend against something horrible; I don't know what. I talk incessantly while we eat, even though he only responds with one-syllable words. I'm anxious that he will say or do something terrible, irreversible, something he never said or did before. When I get his attention, my heart slows a bit, and I'm able to breathe easy again, until there's another pause in the conversation. I talk about all kinds of things: about when Mrs Jensen, after I showed her a drawing that Ernst Hansen did of me, said, Is that drawn by hand? I talk about my mother, about her blood pressure which is too high now, though before it had always been too low. I talk about my book which has been returned from Gyldendal with a strange response, insinuating that I have been reading too much Freud. I don't even know who Freud is. Now I've sent the book to a new publisher by the name of Athenæum, and every day I look forward to hearing a response. One evening Viggo F. notices my restlessness and says that I've turned into quite a chatterbox. I tell him I'm not feeling all that well and that I think there's something wrong with my heart. Nonsense, he laughs, not at your age. It must be some kind of anxiety. He gives me a worried look and asks if anything is bothering me. I assure him there's nothing wrong, that I'm snug as a bug in a rug. Then he says, I'll call Geert Jørgensen and make an appointment for you. He is a head psychiatrist. I saw him myself once many years ago. A very sensible man.

So I sit across from the doctor, a large knobby man with huge eyes that look like they are about to leave their sockets. I tell him everything. I tell him about Piet Hein and about not telling Viggo F. that I want to get divorced. Geert Jørgensen smiles at me cheerfully, while he plays with a letter opener on the desk.

Isn't it, he says, quite interesting to be caught between two different men?

Yes, I say, surprised; because it is.

You have to let Møller go, he says matter-of-factly. It's a crazy marriage. As you may know, I'm the head psychiatrist at Hareskov Sanatorium. I'll recommend to your editor that you stay there for a little while. Then I'll take care of the rest. As soon as you're out of his sight, your heart trouble will pass.

Right then and there he calls Viggo F., who has nothing against the idea. The very next day I pack my suitcase and go to Hareskov, where I get a private room with a view out to the woods. I talk to the head doctor again, who says that Piet Hein may not visit me before everything is taken care of. He'll call Piet and tell him to stay away. At the sanatorium there are only women my mother's age, very dainty and well dressed. I feel weighed down by my shabby clothes, while I think about all the outfits Piet has given me that I can't use yet. The days pass without drama, and my heart returns to normal. I rent a typewriter from a shop in Bagsværd, and with it I write a poem:

> The Eternal Triangle
>
> In my life there are two men
> who cross my path incessantly –
> the one man is the man I love,
> and the other man loves only me.

But I don't really know if I love Piet Hein, just as he has never said that he loves me. He sends me chocolates and letters, and one day he sent me an orchid in a cardboard box. I placed it in a narrow vase and set it on the nightstand without giving it a second thought. On the day that Viggo F. has to go and talk to Dr Jørgensen, he first comes up to my room. He barely says hello before he sees the orchid. He gets pale and sits down on the edge of a chair. Shocked, I see his lower lip trembling. That there, he says, his voice shaking, pointing at the orchid. Who sent that? Is there someone else?

Uh, no, I say immediately. It was sent anonymously, from some secret admirer.

While I say that, I'm thinking of my mother, whose quickness with a remark I have admired my whole childhood.

4

Now it's fall, and I'm wearing a black coat with an ocelot collar while I walk around in the woods. I walk by myself, because my world seems completely different from that of the other women. I only have superficial conversations with them at mealtimes. Piet Hein visits me every day. He brings me chocolate or flowers, and we walk around in the woods for hours, while he tells me how he is looking for a good boarding house for me, and what a great job I did getting rid of Viggo F. I don't feel like I've gotten rid of him just because I don't see him anymore, but I can't explain that to Piet, who is practical, worldly and unsentimental. He kisses me as if he were my happy owner under the multicolored trees whose leaves float down over us, and he doesn't think I look as happy as I ought to. I showed him a letter I received from Viggo F., but Piet just laughed and said what else could we expect from a disappointed, bitter man. Viggo F. had written: Dear Tove, I have received a message from the publisher that they have accepted your book. I am enclosing the accompanying check. And then his signature. I turned the paper over and over, but there was nothing else. The letter upset me, even though I was glad that they wanted my book. It upset me because I'm thinking back on our last good evening, and what we had together, which is now ruined. Dr Jørgensen tells me that Viggo F. doesn't want to get divorced, because he thinks I'll regret what I'm doing with Piet Hein. Viggo F. never liked Piet because of his sarcastic nature, and they only met one another a few times. I got a letter from Ester too. She wrote that they miss me in the club, and she asked me if I would mind if she acts as chairperson in my absence. She couldn't get Viggo F. to reveal where I was, but by twisting stone-faced Piet's arm she was able to obtain my address. If I had been home with Viggo F., I would have paid for dinner at an expensive restaurant to celebrate the occasion. But I don't feel like treating Piet to dinner, because it's hanging in the air that he should be the one to treat me. And I think uneasily about my future, because there was a kind of security in those green rooms. There was security in the thought of being a married woman, who went shopping and made dinner every day, and now it's all ruined. Piet never talks about getting married, and doesn't seem to care if Viggo F. wants to get divorced or not.

Eventually Piet locates a suitable boarding house and I move in with a renewed feeling of being a young girl whose existence is fragile, fleeting and unsure. I have a nice bright room with good furniture, and I'm tended to by a maid with a cap on her head. I bought a typewriter with my advance and I'm transcribing poems on it, because I've started writing poetry again. Piet says I should try selling them to one of the magazines that publish things like that, but I'm afraid they won't accept them. In the evening, when Piet and I lie talking in my narrow bed, I think how strange it is that he never says a single word about himself. His eyes are dull as raisins, and when he smiles, all his clean white teeth show. I still don't know if I'm in love with him. I feel weighed down by the thought that he's just amusing me, while I'm longing for a home and a husband and a child just like all young women do. The boarding house is located on River Boulevard and members of the club come up often and visit me when they are in the area. Then we have coffee, which I order by pushing a button. We talk about Otto Gelsted's lecture at the club. It was about the political engagement of artists, and the discussion fell flat, because none of us are politically engaged. Morten Nielsen sits on the edge of my divan with his hands supporting his big angular face like a cradle. He says, Maybe I should join the freedom fighters. I think it's a stupid idea, because the occupying forces are so powerful, but I don't say that I don't agree. Maybe I've inherited my father's dislike of God, king and homeland, because I don't have the urge to hate the German soldiers tramping around the streets. I'm too busy with my own life, my own uncertain future, to be able to think patriotically right now. I miss Viggo F. and I forget that it made me sick to be in the same room with him. I miss showing him my poems and I'm jealous of my friends who visit him and show him their writing. But the head psychiatrist said that I should leave him alone. One day Ester visits me and says that she has agreed to be Viggo F.'s housekeeper. She got fired from the pharmacy where she worked because she was always late, so she's glad. She's written half a novel, which now she hopes to have time to finish. She says that since I moved out, Viggo F. can't stand being alone.

After I lived in the boarding house for a month, Piet visited me one afternoon. He seemed excited and a bit nervous. He didn't kiss me as usual, but he sat down, drumming lightly on the floor with the silver-handled walking cane that he had picked up recently. There is something I have to tell you, he says, looking at me askance with his raisin eyes. He hangs the cane on the back of the chair and wrings his hands, as if he's cold or is relishing something. He says, I'm sure you'll take this on the chin, won't you? I promise to take it on the chin, but his entire manner frightens me. In this moment he seems like a complete stranger who has never held me in his arms. Quickly he continues, I met a young woman recently, very pretty, very rich. We fell in love immediately, and now she's invited me over to Jylland – to a mansion. It's in her family. I'm leaving tomorrow; I hope you're not upset.

I feel dizzy – what about my rent and what about my future? No tears, he says, opening his hands in an authoritative motion. For God's sake, take it with a stiff upper lip. We're under no obligation here, right? I'm unable to answer, but it feels as if the walls are starting to lean in, and I want to hold them back. My heart is pounding violently like it did back when I felt sick with Viggo F. Before I can say or do anything, Piet is out the door again, so fast it's as if he left through the wall. Then the tears come. I lie down on the divan, sobbing into the pillow, thinking about Nadja and how I should have listened to her warnings. It's hard to stop crying, so maybe that means I was in love with him after all.

Then there's a knock on the door and Nadja walks in, wearing a dingy trench coat over long pants. She sits down calmly on the divan and strokes my hair. Piet asked me to look in on you, she says. Stop crying; he's not worth it. I dry my eyes and stand up. You're right, I say. It was exactly like he did to you. And the chin? she asks, laughing. Were you supposed to take it on the chin? I laugh too, and the world gets a bit brighter. Yes, I say, with a stiff upper lip. He's so funny. Yes he is, admits Nadja, and there's something about him that girls fall for, but then afterwards they have no idea what it was. Afterwards all you can do is laugh at him. She sits there with a pensive look on her benevolent face with its heavy Slavic features. He writes good letters, she says. I've saved all of them. Did he write to you too? Oh yes, I say, walking to the dresser. I take out a whole bundle of letters that I've tied up with a red bow. Let me see them, says Nadja, if you don't mind? I give them to her, and she reads a couple of lines of the first one and immediately throws her head back and starts laughing, so she can hardly stop. Oh God, she says, reading: Dear Kitten, You are the only girl I could ever think of marrying. That is so insane, she says, gasping for air, that is exactly the same thing he wrote to me. She reads some more and realizes that it is word for word the same letter she has at home. You know what, she says, he must have them duplicated someplace. Heaven knows how many Kittens he has, spread around the country. When he leaves that mansion woman, he'll send you there to comfort her. I get serious again and explain to Nadja that I can't stay living here, because it's too expensive, and I'm flat broke. Then she suggests, just like Piet, that I try and sell my poems, because she thinks it would be too sad if I had to work in an office again. Go over to the *Red Evening Post*, she says. Piet sold them a ton of poems, all the ones the *Politiken* didn't want. You have to live by the pen now. All that about being taken care of is nonsense. That must be something you were brought up with.

The next day I visit the editor's office with three poems. I'm shown in to the editor, an old man with a long white beard. While he reads the poems, he pats me on the behind, absent-mindedly and mechanically. Then he says, These are good. You can go out to accounting and withdraw thirty kroner. After that I sell poems to the *Politiken*'s magazine and to Hjemmet, and I write a column for Ekstra Bladet about the

Young Artists Club. So I'm able to stay in the boarding house. Through Ester I learn that Viggo F. is missing me terribly, and that she has to sit and talk with him for hours every night before he goes to bed. I ask her to ask him if he wants to see me, but he doesn't. He doesn't even want her to mention me. I miss him more than I miss Piet Hein, and apart from the sporadic visits by my friends from the club, I never see anyone.

One evening Nadja comes over, dressed, as usual, as if she had just escaped a burning house. You need a circle of friends, she says. You're so alone in the world. I know some young people, out by the south harbor, who would love to meet you. They're all students at Høng Business School, and on Saturday they're having a party. Won't you come? The most charming of them is the dean's son. His name is Ebbe, and he looks just like Leslie Howard. He's twenty-five, and he's studying economics, when he's not drinking. I used to be totally infatuated with him, but he never knew it. He's attracted to poetic, blonde, long haired girls like you. Now listen to me, I say, you're acting like a matchmaker or something. I'll come on Saturday, because you're right, I do need to get out with other young people who aren't artists. I happily prepare my divan, and I go to bed with a faint yearning in my heart to be lying with someone's arm around me. I think about this Ebbe fellow before I fall asleep. I wonder what he looks like? Would he really fall for someone like me? The streetcars roll by, whining through the night, as if they were driving across my living room. People are sitting inside them, going out to have fun, completely normal people, who want to place glorious events between the evening and the morning, when they have to get up early for work. Apart from my writing I'm completely normal too, dreaming about a normal young man, who is attracted to blonde, long-haired girls.

5

On the way out to the south harbor, Nadja tells me a little about 'The Lantern Club', as they call themselves, no one knows why. It's made up of students who have come to Copenhagen to get their degrees from Høng Business School, but they don't do much other than hold parties, get drunk, and lie around with hangovers. We're riding our bicycles into the wind; it's rainy and cold. I'm dressed up as a little girl, with a short dress, a bow in my hair, knee socks and flats. I have a wool sweater over my dress, and over that a trench coat just like Nadja's, with a red scarf around my neck with the ends trailing behind me. That's supposed to be in fashion this year. Nadja is dressed as an Apache girl, and her long black silk pants flap against the bike chain guard with loud smacks. She tells me this group is very freethinking. They're all dirt poor and only get a little money from home. The party will be at Ole and Lise's, who are married with an infant. Ole is going to be an architect, and Lise works in an office, while her mother, who is a widow and lives next door to them, watches the baby. They live off mushrooms from the landfill, she says, which is nearby. She also says that it's a potluck dinner, but that girls don't have to bring anything. They don't let any new men into the group, she says, but they always need girls. When we arrive, everyone is sitting around a table in a long bright room with fine old furniture. They're eating open-faced rye-bread sandwiches – most of them topped with ramona, a kind of carrot mixture with a poisonous color. They are also drinking pullimut, because that is the only alcohol anyone can get. The mood is already pretty high, and everyone is talking at the same time. I say hello to Lise, a pretty, thin girl with a madonna-like face. She welcomes me and then they sing an invented song with unintelligible references to everyone there. Ole stands up and delivers a speech. He has a flat, dark, immense face with two deep furrows from his nose to his mouth, which make him look much older than he is. He is constantly pulling up his pants, as if they were too big for him, and he isn't dressed up like the rest of us. He says he's proud to have a writer in the house, and he says he's sorry that Ebbe is at home with his mother, nursing a fever of 39°C. He just caught the flu. Then the table is moved to the side, and Nadja and Lise carry out the dishes. The record player is turned on, and we start dancing. I dance with Ole, who stoops over me, pulls up his pants, gives a shy laugh and says that he'll go over and get Ebbe. Ebbe lives across the street, and Ole says that Ebbe has been looking forward to meeting me. He says that a little fever won't stand in the way. Then he and another guy go out into the night to bring back Ebbe. The mood is quite loose; everyone is a bit drunk. Lise comes over and asks if I want to see the baby, and we go into the baby's room. It's a six-month-old boy, and I feel a pang of jealousy when she starts nursing him. She's no older than I am, and I feel like I've been wasting my time, since I don't have a baby too. The little boy has a slight shadowed hollow in the back of his neck, just under his hairline. It pulses rhythmically as he drinks. Suddenly the door opens; it's Ole, standing there pulling on his curly black hair. Ebbe's here, he says. Tove, don't you want to say hello? I go with Ole into the living room, where the noise is tremendous. A cover from a record is hanging from the chandelier, and streamers of all different colors are intertwined between the furniture and dangling from the shoulders and hair of the people dancing. Standing in the center there's a young man wearing a blue robe over striped pajamas, and a gigantic scarf is wrapped several times around his neck. This is Ebbe, says Ole proudly, and I shake Ebbe's hand, which is sweaty with fever. He has a drawn, gentle face with fine features, and I get a strong feeling that he is the leader of their clique. Welcome to the Lantern Club, he says. I hope—Then he looks around with a helpless expression and loses his train of thought. Ole claps him on the back. Don't you want to dance with Tove? he asks. Ebbe looks at me for a second with his slanted eyes. Then he extends his palm and says quietly: *Die Sternen, begehrt Mann nicht.** Bravo, exclaims Ole, no one else in the world could have thought of saying that. Ebbe dances with me anyway. His hot cheek finds mine and our steps get a bit unsteady. Then the others suddenly gather around him, hand him a glass, pull on his robe, and ask about his health. Another guy dances with me, and for a moment I lose sight of Ebbe. The gramophone is blasting, and Ole is sitting in the corner with his ear pressed to a homemade speaker, listening to the BBC broadcast. Now everyone is drunk, and a lot of them are sick. Nadja grabs them one by one, leads them

* 'A man should not covet you, O stars', adapted from Goethe's 'Trost in Tränen'.

to the toilet and holds their heads while they throw up. She loves doing that, says Lise, laughing. Lise is dressed as Columbine, and you can see her large plump breasts beneath all the ruffles. I wonder if it's true that you get a nice bust from nursing, and I dance with Ebbe again, who desires the stars after all, because he suggests that we take a break in another room. We lie down on a bed and he takes me in his arms, as if that is something they just do in this group, with no lead-in maneuvers of any kind. I feel happy and loved for the first time in my life. I stroke his thick brown hair, which curls at his neck, and I look into his strange, slanted eyes, which have brown dots in the blue. He says it's because his mother has brown eyes, and that always comes through in one way or another. He asks if he can come visit me at my boarding house, and I say yes. He reaches down on the floor for a bottle he brought in with us, and we both take a drink from it. Then we fall asleep. Early in the morning I wake up and I don't know where I am. Ebbe is still sleeping, and his short, turned-up eyelashes brush lightly against the pillowcase. Suddenly I see another couple in a child's bed by the other wall. They're sleeping in one another's arms and I don't recognize them from the night before. A motley pile of dress-up clothing is lying on the floor. I get up carefully and walk into the living room, which resembles a battlefield. Nadja is already cleaning up, wiping up vomit in the corners. She looks cheerful. That damned pullimut, she says. No one can take it. Isn't he sweet – Ebbe – completely different than that creep Piet. In the baby's room, Lise is sitting, nursing. Watch out for Ebbe, she says smiling, looking up at me. He's a heartbreaker.

I put on my trench coat, tie the red scarf around my neck, and walk in to say goodbye to Ebbe. Oh God, my head, he moans. As soon as I get over this flu I'll come and visit you.

Are you a little bit crazy about me? I say yes, and he apologizes for not walking me out. I can see he's flushed with fever and I say that's perfectly all right. Then I ride my bike home alone. It's not quite daylight yet. The birds are chirping as if it were spring, and I'm thinking, happily, that a college student is in love with me. I have a funny feeling that it might last a lifetime.

When Ebbe is over the flu, he starts coming to visit me every evening, and I neglect the club meetings, because I don't want to miss him. He never stays overnight, because he's afraid of his mother. She's the widow of the college dean. Ebbe has an older brother who also lives at home and can't bring himself to move out, even though he's twenty-eight. When Ebbe leaves, he winds his long scarf so many times around his neck that it reaches all the way up to his nose, because we're having a bitterly cold winter. I get wool in my mouth when he kisses me goodbye.

I start visiting Lise and Ole quite frequently, and I visit Ebbe's mother too. She is little and old, and she describes everything as if it were a problem. Now that my husband is dead, she says, I only have my two boys. She looks at me with her vibrant black eyes, apparently afraid that I am going to take one of the boys away from her. Ebbe's brother's name is Karsten. He's studying to be an engineer and he's always speculating about how he's going to tell his mother that he wants to move out, but he doesn't have the courage. Ebbe's mother is the daughter of a Lutheran priest and she asks me if I believe in God. When I say no, she looks at me sadly and says: Ebbe doesn't either. I hope you both will turn your souls toward the Lord. Ebbe looks embarrassed when she says things like that.

When Ebbe and I go to bed he never uses protection. I've

told him that I want to have a baby, and that I'll take care of it. Every month I put a red cross on my calendar, but time passes and nothing happens. Then my novel comes out, and the next morning my landlord comes running in with the *Politiken*. You're in the paper today, she says, panting. Something about a book. Read it. I open up the paper and I can't believe my eyes. In the most prominent position in the newspaper, next to the 'Day to Day' column, Frederik Schyberg has a review across two columns. The title reads: 'Refined Innocence'. It's an effusive review, and I am giddy with joy. Soon afterwards a telegram arrives from Morten. It reads: Thank goodness for Schyberg and the real genius. Later in the day Morten comes by in person, and while we drink coffee he says that rumors are flying at the club. People are saying I used Viggo F. for a while and then dumped him when I could take care of myself. I tell Morten there is something to that, but it still makes me feel bad, because it's not the whole truth. The next day there's a grook about me in the *Politiken*. It reads:

> I do not swing my poet's hat
> for just any Tove this or that
> but I am thoroughly charmed
> An undebatable debut
> and such great prospects in view
> that I'm afraid a child was harmed.

Evidently he still thinks about his Kitten. But he married his mansion woman and he never comes to the club anymore.

Suddenly, nothing else matters, because I'm a few days late. I discuss it with Lise, who tells me to go to the doctor with a urine sample and have it tested. The doctor promises to call when the results come in, and over the following days

I hardly leave the telephone. Finally he calls and tells me in a totally normal voice: the result was positive. I'm going to have a baby. I can hardly believe it. A tiny clump of mucus inside me is going to expand and grow every day, until I get fat and shapeless like Rapunzel was when I was a child. Ebbe isn't nearly as happy as I am. We have to get married, he says, and I'd better tell my mother. I ask if he has anything against us getting married and he says, No, it's just that we're so young and we have no place to live. He gets a helpless look in his eyes at the thought of all the things to consider, and I kiss his fine, delicate mouth. I feel like I have enough strength for all three of us. Then I realize that I'm not even divorced yet, and I write a nice letter to Viggo F. asking him for a divorce since I'm pregnant. Offended, he writes back: I only have one thing to say: Good grief! Go to a lawyer and get it done, and the sooner the better. When I show the letter to Ebbe, he says: He's ridiculous. What did you ever see in him?

In the following weeks, Ebbe is often drunk when he comes to visit me. He unwinds his scarf with stiff movements, and his tongue wags nonsensically when he tries to say something. I'm no good, he says. You deserve someone better. I haven't told my mother yet. Finally he pulls himself together and tells her. She cries as if it were a disaster and says that now she has nothing to live for. Lise says that Ebbe can't bear tears or reproaches. She says that he's a good but weak person, and that I'm the one who will have to call the shots in our marriage. Even though I don't do anything about it, I don't like hearing that. And besides, I have morning sickness and I throw up every morning. Nadja visits me and says things even more directly. Ebbe is a lush, she says, and he doesn't do a thing. He is terribly sweet, but I'm afraid you're going to be providing for him.

6

We move into a room at Ebbe's mother's house until the divorce is finalized, because we want to be together all the time. Ebbe spends the mornings at the State Pricing Advisory, where a lot of students kill time and earn a little pocket money. He sits with another economics student named Victor. Ebbe has as many friends as there are stars in the sky, and I will never meet all of them. When he and Victor arrive at work in the morning, they sing the psalm of the day from a hymnal booklet which they then use to roll their cigarettes. Finding tobacco is very difficult, and sometimes they roll their cigarettes with ersatz tea. Meanwhile, I'm writing my next novel. I have recently submitted the manuscript of a poetry collection called *Little World*. Ebbe thought of the title. He's quite interested in my work. He wanted to get a degree in literature, but his father, who died two years ago, said that that was a peasant's fantasy. So now he's studying economics, which doesn't interest him in the least. But he loves literature, and he's always reading novels when we're not talking together. He introduces me to books that I never knew existed. And every afternoon when he returns from work, he wants to see what I've written. If he critiques it, there's always substance to his advice, and I follow it. I don't see my family much these days. My brother has moved in with a divorced woman who has a three-year-old child. Ebbe and I visited them, but he and Ebbe don't have much in common. Ebbe is an upper-class young man from the suburbs, and Edvin is a Copenhagen painter's helper, who breathes cellulose lacquer into his damaged lungs every day because he has no other choice. My parents' world is also very remote from Ebbe's. Ebbe talks with my father about books, and with my mother about me, just like Viggo F. used to do. But there's nothing condescending in Ebbe's attitude to them. After we've finished eating dinner with his mother and Karsten, we lie on the bed in our room, talking about the future, about the baby we are going to have, about life, and about our past before we knew one another. Ebbe loves questions that have no definitive answer. For example, he has a theory of why Negroes are black, and another one about why Jews have hooked noses. Once he propped himself up on his elbow and stared at me with an expression of moral intensity. I'm thinking, he said solemnly, about joining the underground resistance. It's not looking so good after the fall of France. I say that he can leave that to people who don't have a wife and child to think of. He seems to forget about the idea. I feel good these days: I'm going to get married, I'm going to have a baby, I'm in love with a young man, and soon we're going to have our own home. I tell Ebbe that I'll never leave him, and that I can't stand it when life gets so complicated, like it's been recently. He lifts my chin and kisses me. It could be, he says, that if you're complicated, your life gets to be like that too.

Finally the divorce goes through, and we rent an apartment

on Tartinisvej, near Lise and Ole and Ebbe's mother. The south harbor is at the end of long Enghavevej like a nail on the end of a finger. This neighborhood is also called 'Music Town' because all the roads are named after composers. The apartment buildings are not very tall, and most of them have little yards out front with grass and trees. Between the last road and open country lies the landfill, and when the wind is just right, the stench carries to the apartments, so we can't keep our windows open. Across from the house where Lise and Ole live, on Wagnervej, there are lots of cabins where people live all year round. One of the cabin ladies cleans Lise's house. And every Saturday, Lise takes the lady's five children upstairs to the bathroom and soaps and scrubs them clean, so the apartment fills with their drawn-out cries. Lise does things like that without thinking twice, and she reminds me of Nadja that way. Nadja has moved in with a sailor who's a communist, and now she's constantly airing communist views, though she was very conservative back when she was seeing Piet. I know this from Ebbe, because I don't go out in the evenings anymore. I'm too tired by eight o'clock because of my pregnancy.

Our apartment is a room and a half, and our full-size bed covers nearly the entire half-room floor. We got the bed from Ebbe's mother. Ebbe's father's desk stands in the other room, along with a dining-room table we bought used, four chairs that we got from Lise, and a divan along one wall. Over the divan we lay a brown blanket, and in a moment of inspiration, Ebbe hangs another brown blanket on the wall behind it. He got a piece of red felt from Lise, and he cut a heart out of it. He glued the heart onto the hanging blanket and stood back to admire his work. In our house, he says, we'll never have drinking parties. Out of consideration for his mother, we aren't moving into our apartment until we're married. Otherwise she would think our sinfulness was too overt.

We're getting married on one of the first days of August, and we ride our bicycles to City Hall holding hands. We arrive too early, so we walk over to Frascati and have coffee. While we drink it, I sit there observing Ebbe's face and I think there is something soft and naive about it, something defenseless, so I feel like protecting him. Suddenly I say: Your top lip really sticks out. I don't mean anything hurtful by it, but he looks at me belligerently. It doesn't stick out any more than yours, he says. Insulted, I say, Mine hardly sticks out at all. Yours covers almost your whole face. His face turns red with anger. Don't criticize my looks, he says. The girls in school were crazy about me. Lise only married Ole because I wasn't interested in her. Irritated, I say, You are so conceited. Meanwhile I'm thinking in wonder: we're fighting, and we've never done that before. Silently Ebbe pays the waiter. His dark jacket sleeves are too long; he borrowed his wedding suit from his brother. In the Lantern Club they don't wear shabby clothes because they're poor; it's because being well-dressed is seen as ludicrous. Ebbe runs his index finger around his stiff collar, which is also too big, and he walks in front of me with long strides, back to City Hall, without saying a word. Then he stops and flips his hair back with a toss of his head. He says, If you don't take back that thing about my top lip, I won't marry you. I start to laugh. No, I say, that's too childish. Are we seriously going to become enemies over whose top lip sticks out more? It can be mine then. I pull my top lip down over my bottom lip and try to stick out my eyes so I can see it. It's a half-mile long, I say. Come on, we're going to get married.

And we do. We move into the apartment and we hire a woman to clean, because I'm starting to earn a lot of money.

Her name is Mrs Hansen, and when she comes to interview for the job, Ebbe says emphatically, Can you peel carrots? She says she thinks she can. Ebbe explains to her that carrots are very healthy, considering so many things are unavailable now. Since then she has always been amused that there are never any carrots in the house. The days pass like a drumroll before a solo. I read books about pregnancy, motherhood and caring for an infant, and I can't understand why Ebbe isn't as interested in all of this as I am. He says he almost can't believe that he's going to be a father. He also can't believe it when he sees my name in the newspaper. He doesn't understand that he's gotten married to a famous person, and he doesn't know if he likes it. Twisting his hair around his fingers, Ebbe sits in the evening solving equations. He loves when they work out and he says that he probably should have been a mathematician. I tell him that Geert Jørgensen once said to me that no normal man would ever find me attractive. Ebbe says, So who's normal? while he pats his pockets to find his notebook or his tobacco pouch or his keys. He is quite absent-minded and is always losing his things. He walks with his head bent back, as if he is trying to keep his eyes focussed and his chin up, so he frequently trips over things on the street. He often goes to parties at Ole and Lise's, and he comes home drunk and wakes me up in the middle of the night. I get angry and brush him away, because I really need my sleep these days. He always apologizes the next day. Sometimes I go to visit my mother, or she visits me. I talk with her about giving birth, and she says that Edvin and I were born in a cloud of soap bubbles, because she tried to force us to come out by eating pine-oil soap. She says, I never liked children.

The days pass, weeks pass, months pass. I'm going to give birth at Dr Aagaard's private clinic at Hauser Square, and I have my checkups with him. He's a nice older man who eases my many anxieties about the birth. I'm told that I should come back when there are five minutes between contractions. But the due date passes and nothing happens. I bought a sealskin coat, and I have to keep moving the buttons farther and farther out until they're dangling on the very edge of the jacket. Ebbe has to tie my shoes for me, since I can't reach them. I don't think I've ever seen a pregnant woman as fat as me. I'm afraid that I'm going to have a huge baby with water on the brain. I read about that somewhere. Often I borrow Lise's little boy Kim and take him for walks. He's sweet and laughs a lot, and I think about the poem by Nis Petersen: I collect the smiles of little children. In the middle of all this I get interviewed by Karl Bjarnhof for the *Social-Demokraten*. I get a shock when I see the headline: 'I want money, power and fame'. Did I really say that? The entire interview gives an unflattering impression of me. I'm portrayed as a vain, ambitious and superficial person, who only thinks about herself. Otherwise journalists have always treated me well, and I wonder what I could have done to Karl Bjarnhof. Then I remember that he's one of Viggo F.'s friends, so maybe he's angry because I left Viggo F.

This winter is very cold, and there's a layer of ice on the streets. I feel impatient, waiting for the contractions to start, so to bring them on I run, arm in arm with Ebbe, panting around the house after dark. The buttons on my coat spring open; nothing else happens. Finally one morning I have a stomachache and I ask Mrs Hansen if it could be contractions. She thinks it probably is, and it gets worse as the day progresses. Ebbe holds my hand as the contractions come. That evening we go to the clinic and he says goodbye with a sad, helpless expression.

*

She's so ugly, I say, surprised, looking down at the little bundle of a baby in my arms. Her face is pear-shaped, with two dark marks on her temples from the forceps. There's not a hair on her head. The doctor laughs. That's just because you've never seen a newborn baby before, he says. They're never cute, but the mother usually thinks so anyway. I'll call your husband now. Ebbe arrives with a bouquet of roses in his hand. He's carrying them awkwardly, and I realize that he's never given me a gift before. Then he sits down next to me and looks into the cradle, where they've put the baby. She's pretty chubby, he says, and I feel offended. I say, Is that all you have to say? The birth took twenty-four hours, and I swore I would never have a baby again. I yelled and screamed in pain, and all you have to say is that she's chubby? Ebbe looks ashamed and makes it even worse by saying that maybe she'll get prettier as she grows. Then he asks when I'm coming home, because he misses me. I bend over the cradle and touch the tiny fingers. I say, Now we are a father, mother and child – a normal, regular family. Ebbe asks, Why do you want to be normal and regular? Everyone knows you're not. I don't know how to answer him, but I have wanted that as far back as I can remember.

7

Something terrible has happened. Ever since Helle was born I've lost all desire to go to bed with Ebbe, and when I do it anyway I feel absolutely nothing. I tell Dr Aagaard about it, and he says that it's not unusual – I'm just drained from nursing, child-rearing and working like a madwoman, so there's nothing left over for Ebbe. But it makes Ebbe unhappy, because he thinks it's his fault. He talks it over with Ole, who advises him to buy van de Velde's *Ideal Marriage*. He buys it and reads it blushing, because this book is the present-day pornographic bible. He reads about all the positions and we try a new one every night. In the morning we're both sore from attempting to be acrobats, and it doesn't help in the least. I talk about it with Lise, who tells me confidentially that she never got anything out of sex before she had Kim. She looks at me thoughtfully with her gentle madonna-eyes: How about taking a lover? she asks. Sometimes it brings a couple together if one of them has someone else. She has a lover herself – a lawyer. He works at the police station, and they walk around together every day for hours, while she tells Ole that she's working overtime. Ole knows, but then doesn't know at the same time. Ole has had a child by another woman, and before the child was born Lise thought seriously about adopting it. Then it turned out the baby was deaf and dumb, so now she's glad she didn't do it. I tell her I don't want a lover, because I won't be able to work if my life becomes all messy and complicated again. And I realize more and more that the only thing I'm good for, the only thing that truly captivates me, is forming sentences and word combinations, or writing simple, four-line poetry. And in order to do this I have to be able to observe people in a certain way, almost as if I needed to store them in a file somewhere for later use. And to be able to do this I have to be able to read in a certain way too, so I can absorb through all my pores everything I need, if not for now, then for later use. That's why I can't interact with too many people; and I can't go out too much and drink alcohol, because then I can't work the next day. And since I'm always forming sentences in my head, I'm often distant and distracted when Ebbe starts talking to me, and that makes him feel dejected. This, together with all the attention I give to Helle, makes him feel like he's being abandoned, outside my world, where he used to be included. When he comes home in the afternoon he still likes reading what I've written, but now his comments have become meaningless and unfair, as if he's trying to hit me in my sorest spot. One day we start arguing, because in my book *The Street of Childhood*, there's a character named Mr Mulvad who likes to solve mathematical equations, and Ebbe is furious. That's me, he says. All my friends will recognize it and laugh at me. He demands that I remove Mr Mulvad from the book. It's true that Mr Mulvad is a strange fish, because I'm not that skilled at characterizing men yet. But I don't want to delete him. I don't understand, says Ebbe. Why can't you make your characters like Dickens did, for example. You take yours from real life. That's not art. I ask him to stop reading what I write, since he doesn't understand it anyway. He says he's sick and tired of being married to a writer, who's frigid on top of everything. I gasp for air and break down in tears. I've never fought with anyone since I fought with my brother back when we were children, and I can't stand being at odds with Ebbe. Helle wakes up crying, and I pick her up. Can't he solve equations, I say pitifully. Otherwise I don't know what a guy like that would do in his free time. Ebbe puts his arms around me and Helle together and says, I'm sorry, Tove. Please stop crying. He can solve equations, and I didn't mean what I said. It's just bothering me, that's all.

One afternoon, not long after that fight, Ebbe doesn't come home at the usual time, and I realize how dependent I am on him. I pace the floor and I'm unable to do anything productive. Ebbe goes out often in the evenings, but he always comes home first. As it gets later, I nurse Helle, get her dressed and go over to see Lise, who has just come home from work. She says Ole isn't home either, and that they're probably out together. Then they probably met some other friends and lost their way home. It wouldn't be the first time that had happened. You're so conventional, she says, smiling. Maybe you should have married the kind of man who always comes right home with his paycheck and never drinks. Then I tell her about our fight and I say that our marriage isn't going so well anymore. I confide in her that I'm afraid he's going to find someone else; someone who isn't a writer and isn't frigid. He might do that for one night, she says, but Ebbe would never dream of leaving you and Helle. He is really proud of you; it's obvious when he talks about you. You just have to understand that it's so easy for him to feel inferior. You're famous, you earn money, you love your work. Ebbe's just a poor student who's being more or less supported by his wife. He's studying for a degree he doesn't fit, and he has to get drunk to cope with life. But it will be a relief when your sex life gets going again. And it will; you're just exhausted from nursing. She picks Kim up onto her lap and starts playing with him. When Ole graduates, she says, I want to become a child psychologist. I can't stand working in an office. Lise loves other people's children as well as her own. She loves other people in general, and friends are always coming by and confiding things in her they wouldn't tell even the people closest to them. When do you think he'll come home? I ask. I don't know, she says. Once Ole was gone for eight days, but then I started to get nervous. After putting Kim to bed, Lise sits with her legs pulled up and her chin on one knee. Her entire person radiates peace and friendship, and I feel a bit better. Sometimes, I say, I don't think I can deal with other people at all. It's as if all I can see in the whole world is myself. That's nonsense, says Lise. You really do love Ebbe. I say, Yes, I do, but not in the right way. If he forgets his scarf, I don't remind him. I don't go out of my way to make nice food for him or anything like that. I think I can only like other people if they're interested in me; that's why I'll never suffer from unrequited love. That might be so, she says, but Ebbe is interested in you. I tell her about Mr Mulvad and the equations, and she starts laughing. I didn't know Ebbe solved equations; that's funny. I say, No, that's not what I mean. When I'm writing I don't care about anyone. I can't. Lise says that artists have to be self-centered, and that I shouldn't think about it so much. I walk home through the pitch-black streets, which the stars don't have the power to brighten. I'm glad I have the baby carriage to lean on. It's not quite eight o'clock, and I'm hurrying because that's the curfew. Everyone is supposed to be home by eight. That means Ebbe won't be coming home tonight, wherever he is. I change Helle, put her in pajamas and tuck her into bed. She's four months old and she gives me a toothless smile, while clutching my finger with her whole hand. It's a good thing that, for now, she doesn't care if her father is home or not.

The next morning Ebbe comes home in terrible shape. His jacket is buttoned crooked and his scarf is all the way up to his eyes, even though it's spring and mild weather. His eyes are red from drinking and lack of sleep. I'm so glad to see him alive that I'm not interested in yelling at him. He stands there swaying in the middle of the floor and does a few awkward steps of the 'baboon dance', a solo dance he always does at a certain point in his drunkenness, while everyone around him claps. He stands on one leg and swings around, but loses his balance and reaches for a chair. I cheated on you, he says, in a gravelly voice. Dejected, I say, With who? With a pretty girl, he says, who isn't pregnant, no, fri-frigid. Someone Ole knew from the Tokanten Pub. I ask, Are you going to see her again? Well, he says, plopping down in a chair, that depends on a lot of things. If you make that Mulvad guy play solitaire instead, then maybe I won't see her anymore. Otherwise, I don't know. I walk over to him, remove the scarf from his mouth and kiss him. Don't see her anymore, I say emphatically, I'll have Mulvad play solitaire instead. He hugs me around my waist and lays his head against my groin. I'm a monster, he mumbles. Why do you want to have anything to do with me? I'm poor and a drunk and I'm good for nothing. You're beautiful and famous and you could have anyone you want. But, I say wholeheartedly, we have a child together. I don't want any man but you. He stands up and embraces me.

I'm so tired, he says. I can't solve our problems by getting drunk. That damned van de Velde; it gives me a backache. Then we laugh and I help him out of his clothes and into bed. Then I sit at my typewriter and I forget, while I'm writing, that my husband has gone to bed with someone else. I forget everything, until Helle starts crying because she's hungry.

The next day I write a poem that starts like this: Why does my lover walk in the rain, without a coat and without a hat? Why does my lover leave me at night, no one could understand that. When I show it to Ebbe, he says it's good, but that it wasn't raining, and that he had a coat on. I laugh and tell him about the time Edvin read my poems and said that I was such a liar. Ebbe says that he'll never lose his way home again, since it makes me so miserable. It's the damned pullimut, he says. To get a beer at a pub, you have to buy a glass of pullimut too, and that gets people drunk. I'm jealous and I ask what the girl looked like. He says that she wasn't anywhere nearly as pretty as me. The kind that chases artists and students, he says. There are so many of them you could use them to feed the sharks. He adds: If we hadn't had Helle, everything between us would still be fine. I say, It'll return to normal; I think it's getting better. But it's not true. Something essential, something incredibly good and valuable between us has been destroyed, and it's worse for Ebbe, since he can't just write away his problems and sorrows. Before we fall asleep that night, I stare into his slanted eyes, whose brown dots glow in the light of the lamp. Whatever happens, I say, promise me you won't leave me and Helle. He promises. We'll grow old together, he says. You'll get wrinkles, and the skin under your chin will droop like my mother's, but your eyes will never age. They will always be the same with the black line around the blue. That was what I fell in love with. We kiss and lie in each other's arms, chaste as brother and sister. After the van de Velde period passes, Ebbe doesn't try to have sex with me anymore, even though I'm not opposed to it and I have rarely turned him away.

8

One day at the end of May, Ester visits us. She says the club meetings are falling apart, partly because of the curfew, partly because of unwillingness from the restaurant, for which we haven't exactly been a goldmine, and partly because of complications with the members. Sonja can't seem to finish her novel, which Morten Nielsen edits and edits. She has also let Professor Rubow read a few chapters. Halfdan has a poetry collection coming out from Athenæum, which have also praised Ester's own new novel, which will be published in the fall. I've delivered my manuscript *The Street of Childhood*, and now that I'm not currently writing, I have a huge void inside me that nothing can fill. It feels like everything is going into me but nothing is coming out again. Lise says that now I have to enjoy life for a while, that I deserve it after all that hard work. But for me life is only enjoyable when I'm writing. From sheer boredom I hang out for hours with Arne and Sinne, who live on Schubert Street. They're the couple who were lying in the child's bed, that first night Ebbe and I met. Arne is an economics student like Ebbe, and he gets so much money from home that he doesn't have to work. Sinne is the daughter of a farmer from the Limfjord area, and she is buxom, red-haired and full of energy. She's started studying for an associate's degree, because she can't stand how little she knows. I tell her that I've grown used to my ignorance and that I'm terrible at learning things. I tell her I got divorced from Viggo F. before I ever even finished *The French Revolution*.

Ester doesn't live with Viggo F. anymore. She says she got tired of hearing how much he missed me and how bitter he was that I left him. She moved back home, but that's not so good either. Her father is a bankrupt grocer who brings his lovers home, one after the other. Her mother has gotten used to it. You know what, Ester says, I'm sick and tired of all that forced freethinking. I am too, and I ask her what a couple of weirdos like us should be doing when we aren't writing. Then she tells me her real reason for coming. Back from when she worked at the pharmacy, she knows a painter named Elisabeth Neckelmann. Elisabeth lives with another woman who wears a collar and a suit and uses an amber cigarette holder, because she only likes women. And she likes me, says Ester calmly, and she asked if I might want to live in her vacation home for a while. I think it sounds nice, but I can't live there with Halfdan, because we won't have any income. Would you stay there with me? The country air would be good for Helle. When I hesitate before answering, Ebbe interrupts: I think you should go, he says, a little separation can revitalize a marriage. He adds that he'll have more peace and quiet for studying without Helle bothering him. His exams are soon, and he has a lot of catching up to do. So I agree to Ester's offer. I like her because she's so calm, friendly and sensible, and because she has the same mission in life as I do. Ebbe promises to come visit me there, as often as he can, even though the house is far from Copenhagen, somewhere in southern Sjælland. Ester and I decide to bicycle out there the next day, and in the evening Ebbe goes to bed with me for the first time in a long while. But he does it angrily and uncaringly, as if he's irritated that he's still attracted to me. It'll be different, I say, feeling guilty, after I finish nursing. I get milk on him and he laughs. He says, Yeah, it's not that easy going to bed with a dairy.

The house sits in lowlands, with a wheat field behind it and grass sticking up and wild raspberry canes along the slope up to the road, where a pair of crooked pine trees hide the walk. Inside the house there's a large living room, with an old-style stove at one end, and a little room with two beds, where we lie so close to one another I can hear Ester's quiet breathing if I wake momentarily in the middle of the night. I sleep with Helle and I feel cosy and glad with her warm little body next to mine. During the day she lies in her carriage out in the sunshine, but she doesn't tan, just like me. We both have fair skin. Meanwhile Ester gets a tan within a couple of days. It makes her teeth look like they've become whiter, and the whites of her eyes resemble wet porcelain against her taut brown skin. I wake up first in the morning, because Ester needs more sleep than I do. With lots of difficulty, I light the stove with wood we buy from the farmer nearby, who also sells us milk and eggs. The stove puts out more smoke than fire, and I have to light it several times before it really catches. Then I make tea, and butter some bread, and sometimes I serve Ester breakfast in bed. You're going to spoil me, she says happily, rubbing the sleep out of her fall-brown eyes. Her long black hair falls down over her smooth forehead. The days pass with long walks, talks, and playing with Helle, who has just got her first tooth. I've never been out in the country before, and I'm amazed at the silence, which is like nothing I have ever experienced.

I feel something resembling happiness, and I wonder if this is what is meant by enjoying life. In the evening I go for a walk alone while Ester watches Helle. The aromas from the fields and pine forest are stronger than on the day we arrived. The lighted windows in the farmhouse shine like yellow squares in the darkness, and I wonder what the people there do to pass the time. The man probably sits listening to the radio; and the wife probably darns socks which she pulls up out of a woven basket. Soon they'll yawn and stretch and look out at the weather and say a few words about the work awaiting them in the morning. Then they'll tiptoe to bed so as not to wake the children. The yellow squares will go dark. Eyes will shut all over the world. The cities go to sleep, and the houses, and the fields. When I come back to the house, Ester has made some dinner, like fried eggs or something like that. We don't go to much trouble. Then we light the petroleum lamp and talk for hours, with long pauses in between, which aren't tense and sizzling like the silences between Ebbe and I have become. Ester tells me about her childhood, her unfaithful father and her gentle, patient mother. I tell her about my childhood too, and our pasts come alive between us like a section of a wall teeming with life. These quiet days are only interrupted when Ebbe or Halfdan comes to visit. Sometimes they ride their bicycles out here together, and they arrive hot and panting. We have a nice time while they're here, but I like being alone with Ester better. She's like a boy in her faded short-sleeved shirts and long pants and her pouty mouth with the small, upturned top lip.

On warm mornings we wash all over out by the edge of

the field. Ester's body is brown and strong with large firm breasts. She's a bit taller than I am, with broad shoulders. I squeal when she pours the cold water over me, and my skin turns blue with goose bumps. But Ester doesn't mind at all when it's her turn, and she lets the sun dry her shiny smooth limbs, stretched out in the grass like a crucifix. I think I could live this way for the rest of my life. It's too complicated to think about Ebbe and our constant problems.

The grain is golden, standing there swaying in the wind, heavy with ripe kernels. I'm awakened very early by a cuckoo calling outside the house, first near, then distant, as if amusing itself by teasing us. Finally one of us tumbles out of bed, dizzy with sleep, opens the top half of the Dutch door, and claps to scare it away. An hour later the harvester starts cutting out in the field, and the sun lifts its yellow forehead up behind the pine woods. I lie there looking at Ester while I nurse. I'm thinking that soon we will leave and each go back to our husbands. I think about Ruth too, my childhood friend, and a warm feeling leads my thoughts aimlessly around in space. When Ester wakes up, I ask her, Do you think I should stop nursing? Sure, she says smiling. Helle doesn't seem to be lacking anything, but some solid food wouldn't be bad. Though you'll lose your nice looking bosom.

I come home to a sunburned Ebbe, who passed his first semester with the lowest grades possible; but he made it. He is sincerely glad to see me again, and when he hugs me I can tell that my frigidity is passing. I tell him, and he says, Then nothing in the world will ever come between us again. I don't think it will either. But in the following days I think about Ester's little boyish face with the pouty mouth, and how in some indecipherable way she is the reason that Ebbe and I have become close again.

9

In the fall my new book comes out, and it gets good reviews everywhere except in the *Social-Demokraten*, where Julius Bomholt rips it apart across two columns under the headline: 'Escape from Worker Street'. He writes that the book contains 'not a single glimmer of gratitude'. 'It also lacks', he adds, 'a description of our young healthy boys in the Danish Social Democratic Union (DSU).' I cry into my ersatz tea, blubbering: But I've never met anyone from the DSU so how could I ever describe them? Ebbe does what he can to comfort me, but I'm not used to being criticized like that, and I sob as if a member of my closest family just died. He used to be so nice to me, I say, when Viggo F. and I visited him. Ebbe says that he's probably angry because I left Viggo F., just like Barnhof was, and the review does seem cruel, as if there were a personal grudge behind it. Graham Greene writes somewhere, Ebbe continues, looking up at the ceiling like he always does when he's really thinking, that there is something wrong with a person who has never had a flop. So I let him comfort me. I cut out all the reviews except the bad one, which doesn't matter anyway, and I bring them over to my father. He glues them in my scrapbook, which is already half full. Then he says to me reproachfully, Couldn't you have left out the part about me lying there sleeping with the rear end of my pants worn shiny and turned toward the living room? I am not always asleep and my pants are not worn shiny. My mother says, No one knows that it's you. The mother in the book doesn't resemble me at all. Then she tells me that she lent their copy of my book to a woman from the ice-creamery when she asked her what it was like having a famous daughter. My mother says, Before that she never gave me the time of day.

This is a brief happy period, when Ebbe doesn't go out in the evening and doesn't drink too much. On the other hand, it's not going well between Lise and Ole. They're fighting over pressing financial problems, because Ole has student debt and Lise doesn't earn very much at the department where she works. They would die of starvation if it weren't for the mushrooms from the landfill, which Lise picks at dusk, and she tells me she wants to get a divorce and marry her lawyer. He's married with two children. And Arne wants to divorce Sinne, because she has a lover who sells on the black market and earns fifty kroner a day, an outrageous amount. In the evening I lie in Ebbe's arms and we promise one another that we will never separate and never cheat on each other.

I tell Ebbe that I've always hated change. I tell him how sad I was when we moved from Hedebygade over to Westend where I never felt at home. I tell him that I'm like my father. When my mother and Edvin changed the furniture around at home, my father and I always moved it back. Ebbe laughs and strokes my hair. You're a goddamned reactionary, he says. I am too, even though I'm a radical. Then his gentle, dark voice spins an unending spool of comfort and constancy into my ear.

He's developing his theories about why Negroes are black and why Jews have hooked noses, and about how many stars there are in the sky; unanswerable questions to which I fall asleep like a child to a repetitious lullaby. Outside is the evil complicated world, which we cannot bear and which wants to brush us aside. The police have been taken over by the Germans, and Ebbe has become a CB'er.* It's supposed to be a kind of replacement for the police. They have blue uniforms with slanted shoulders, and Ebbe's uniform cap is too large for him. I think he looks like the Good Soldier Švejk in it, and when he says that he ought to join the resistance, I can't take him seriously.

When Helle is nine months old, panting and grunting with effort, she stands up in her playpen. She grips the bars, swaying and screeching with joy. When I bend over to congratulate and praise her, my mouth starts watering and I have to run and throw up. I tell myself that I probably ate something that didn't agree with me, but the thought that I could be pregnant makes my legs tremble. If that's the case, I know it will ruin everything between Ebbe and me.

You're in the second month, says Dr Herborg, my public-healthcare doctor, and he sits down, while the curtain that is always hanging between me and reality turns gray and perforated, like a spider web. A button is missing from the doctor's shiny white coat, and he has a long black hair sticking out of one of his nostrils. But I don't want to have this baby, I say emphatically. It was a mistake. I must have put my diaphragm in wrong. He smiles and looks at me unsympathetically. Dear

* A member of the Civil og Beskyttelse, the civilian defense and rescue corps formed when the Germans dissolved the Danish police during the occupation.

Lord, he says, how many children do you think are born by mistakes? The mothers love them anyway. I ask carefully, Can't I have it taken out? and immediately the smile disappears from his face like a rubber band gone limp. I do not do that, he says coolly, and you may know that it is illegal. Then I ask him, following Lise's advice, if he can refer me to someone who does do it. No, he says, that is also illegal. So I go and visit my mother, who I know will understand. She's sitting in the kitchen playing solitaire. Oh, she says, when she hears my reason for coming, it's not so hard to knock it out of there. Just go to the pharmacy and buy a bottle of amber oil. Drink it down and that'll work. It's worked for me twice, so I know what I'm talking about. I buy the amber oil and I sit across from my mother on the kitchen chair. When I take the top off the bottle, a nauseating smell surrounds me and I run out to the bathroom and throw up. I can't do it, I say, I can't get that down. My mother doesn't have any other ideas, so I walk to the government office where Lise works and I stand outside against the building, waiting for her. I can see the green roof of the stock exchange, glinting weakly in the twilight, and I remember my walks with Piet through the dark city on the way home from the club meetings. Back then I wasn't pregnant, and if I had stayed with Viggo F. I wouldn't have become pregnant either. People go by without noticing me. Women walk past alone, or holding their children's hands. Their faces are relaxed and introspective, and they probably don't have anything growing inside them that they don't want. Lise, I exclaim as she walks toward me. He won't do it. What in the world am I going to do? On the way to the streetcar I tell her about my mother's horrible amber oil, which is a remedy that Lise has never heard of. I go in with her to pick up Kim from her mother's. Her mother is an authoritative woman wearing a floor-length dress with a cap on her head because she has a bald spot. I recall that she has given birth to ten children, because Lise's father always wanted there to be a baby in the cradle, and no one ever cared what she thought about that. When we're back at Lise's, she says that I mustn't panic; there must be a solution. She's going to ask a young woman at her office who had a pregnancy terminated illegally about a year ago. Unfortunately the woman is sick at the moment, but as soon as she's back at work, Lise will get the address for me. Dr Leunbach isn't doing them right now, says Lise, because he was just in jail for it. Maybe Nadja knows of someone, she says, but I don't remember where she and her sailor live. But I can't just wait around, I say desperately, I have to do something. I can't work, and I've lost all feelings toward Ebbe and Helle. Lise says that there are probably lots of doctors in the same situation as Leunbach. She says that if I have to do something, I could call them one by one from the phone book, and maybe I'll get lucky. In the meantime, the woman from the office might get better; so I shouldn't lose hope. She looks at me solemnly: Do you really think it would be so terrible, she asks, if you had another child? Lise doesn't understand either. I don't want anything to happen to me that I don't want, I say. It's like getting caught in a trap. And our marriage won't be able to bear another period of nursing frigidity. I can't stand it as it is when Ebbe touches me.

When I get home, Ebbe tells me that he's contacted the resistance and he's going to be trained as a freedom fighter, to prepare for the day when the Germans capitulate and pull out of the country. No one thinks it will happen without a fight. No one thinks they're going to win either, not after their defeat at Stalingrad. I could not care less, I tell him irritably, if you want to play soldier; I have other things to deal with. Ebbe says he isn't so crazy about the idea of getting rid of the baby. People can die from that, he says, and in any case he won't help me find a doctor to do it. I can't be bothered to talk to him. He doesn't understand. I don't know what I ever saw in him.

The next day I begin my doctor odyssey. I can only do a couple of visits a day, because they all have consultations at the same times. I sit across from these white coats in my worn-out trench coat with my red scarf around my neck. They look at me coldly and in disbelief: Who in the world took it upon themselves to give you my address? Dear woman, there are women who are much worse off than you. You're married and you only have one child. One of them says, You don't want me to commit a crime, do you? There's the door.

I return home, miserable and humbled. I pick up Helle from Ebbe's mother's house and I nurse her, without paying her any attention. I put her in bed, and then pick her up again. The telephone rings and a voice says, Hello, this is Hjalmar, is Ebbe home? I hand Ebbe the phone, and he answers with one-syllable words. Then he puts on the coat he inherited from his father with the silly strap in the back. He slips on his high rubber boots because it's raining and a cap that he otherwise never wears, pulled down over his forehead. Under his arm he is holding a briefcase uncomfortably, as if it were filled with dynamite. His face is pale. Do I look suspicious? he says. No, I say flatly, though even a child would think there was something fishy about him from miles away. After he leaves, I scan the telephone book some more, page after page. But finding an abortion doctor this way is like trying to find a needle in a haystack, and I give up after a couple of days. I realize I'm in a race against time, because I know no one will do it if I'm more than three months pregnant. It's not easy to see Lise in the evening, because she's with her lawyer after work, and she doesn't think we should ask Ole, because he has the same attitude as Ebbe. Men seem to be excluded from my world right now. They're foreign creatures, it's as if they came from another planet. They're not in touch with their bodies. They don't have any tender, soft organs where a blob of slime can attach itself like a tumor and, completely independent of their volition, start living its own life. One evening I go to visit Nadja's father and ask where she and her sailor live. It's a basement apartment in Østerbro, and I go right over there. They're sitting eating, and Nadja kindly asks if I will join them. But the smell of food makes me nauseous, and I can hardly eat anything these days. Nadja has had her hair cut, and she's affected a swinging gait, as if she were on the deck of a ship. The sailor's name is Einar, and he repeats the same phrases again and again: That's right, that's the way to do it, etc. Nadja talks like that too. When she finds out why I came by, she says that she can get me some quinine pills. She used them for a miscarriage herself once. But it could take a couple of days to work, she says. It's not that easy. But I know where you're coming from, she says. You hate the thought of it growing eyes and fingers and toes and you can't do anything about it. You stare at other children and you don't see any redeeming qualities in them. You can't think of anything but being alone in your own body again.

Slightly relieved, I tell Lise that Nadja has promised to get me some quinine pills, but Lise isn't so enthusiastic. She says, I've heard that some people go blind and deaf from those. I say that I don't care, as long as I get rid of this.

Finally, the young woman we had been waiting for comes back to work at the office, and Lise gets the address of the doctor who helped her. For the first time in a long time I feel happy, walking home with the note in my hand. The man's name is Lauritzen and he lives on Vesterbro Street. People call him 'Abortion-Lauritz', so it must be right. I can look at Helle and Ebbe again. I put Helle on my lap and play with her, and I say to Ebbe: When you go out and meet Hjalmar, don't wear a cap and you should hold that briefcase as if it had books inside. You are so bad at that. But he calms me down by saying that he's not going to be taking part in any sabotage operations, so there's not much chance the Germans will capture him. Tomorrow at this time, I say, I will be happier than I have ever been in my entire life.

The next day I put on the lined fustian jacket that I bought from Sinne, because it's getting cold out. Sinne had it sewn from some old comforters from her family, but when everyone and his brother started wearing fustian jackets, she didn't want it anymore. I'm also wearing long pants. I bicycle to Vesterbro Street, which is already decorated for Christmas with pine garlands and red ribbons along the sidewalk. I've been told not to tell anyone and not to say where I got the address from. There are a lot of people in the waiting room, mostly women. A woman in a fur coat is pacing, wringing her hands. She pats a little girl on the head as if it were something her hands did all on their own, and then she continues pacing. She turns and approaches a young woman and asks, May I please go in before you? I'm in a lot of pain. Okay, says the woman amenably, and when the door to the consultation room opens and someone yells: Next! she runs inside and slams the door shut. A few moments later the woman comes out a changed person. Her eyes are beaming, her cheeks are red, and there is a strange distant smile on her lips. She pulls aside the curtain and looks down at the street. How beautiful, she says, to see all those decorations. I can't wait until Christmas. Amazed, I watch her go. My respect for the doctor has grown. If he can help such a miserable person in just a couple of minutes, who knows what he could do for me.

What seems to be the trouble? the doctor says, looking at me with his tired, friendly eyes. He is an older, gray-haired man with an undefinable, slovenly appearance. There's a salami sandwich on his desk, with both ends of the bread curled up. I tell him that I'm pregnant but that I don't want another baby. Well, he says, rubbing his chin, I'm sorry to disappoint you. I'm not doing that for the time being, because it's getting hot around here.

My disappointment is so immense, so paralyzing, that I bury my face in my hands and burst out crying. But you're my last chance, I sob; I'm almost three months pregnant. If you don't help me, I'll kill myself. That's what so many women say, he says quietly, removing his glasses to get a better look at me. Now, he says, you're Tove Ditlevsen, aren't you? I admit it, but I don't see that it makes any difference. I read your last book, he says, it was good. I'm an old Vesterbro boy myself. If you'll just stop crying, he says very slowly, I might be able to whisper an address to you. I am about to hug him in gratitude when he writes an address down on a slip of paper for me. You can get an appointment with him, he says. All he does is poke a hole in the amniotic sac. If you start to bleed, you have to call me. And if I don't start bleeding? I ask, anxious that this is going to be more complicated than I thought. That wouldn't be good, he says, but it usually does. We'll cross that bridge when we come to it.

When I come home I tell Ebbe about it, and he pleads with me to give up my mission. No, I say vehemently, I would rather die. Ill at ease, he paces the living room, looking at the ceiling as if he could find a convincing argument up there. I call the doctor, who lives in Charlottenlund. Tomorrow six o'clock, he says in a grumpy, toneless voice. Just come right in; the door will be open. Bring three hundred kroner with you. I tell Ebbe not to worry. If anything happens I'll be at the doctor's, so he'll be careful. When it's all over, I say, things will return to normal, Ebbe. That's why I need to have this done.

10

I take the streetcar to Charlottenlund, because I don't want to ride my bicycle, not knowing what kind of condition I'll be in after my appointment. It's two days before Christmas, and people are loaded down with packages covered in bright wrapping paper. Maybe this will all be over by Christmas Eve, so we can have Christmas at my parents' house again. I would love that. I'm sitting next to a German soldier. A heavyset woman with packages has just made a big show of getting up and moving over to the opposite side. I feel bad for the soldier, who probably has a wife and children at home, where he would rather be, instead of traipsing around in a foreign country that his leader decided to invade. Ebbe is sitting at home, more nervous than me. He bought me a flashlight so I can find the address in the dark. We looked in a book to find out what an amniotic sac was. When it breaks, the book said, the water comes out and the birth starts. But there's supposed to be blood, not water. Neither of us really understands.

The doctor greets me in the entry, where a bare lightbulb dangles from a hook in the ceiling. He seems nervous and grouchy. The money, he says flatly, holding out his hand. I give it to him, and he nods toward the examination room. He's about fifty, small and shriveled, and the corners of his mouth droop, as if he has never smiled. Come on up, he says, slapping his hand on the examination table with the hanging straps for patients' legs. I lie down with an anxious glance at the side table which has on it a row of shiny pointed instruments. Will it hurt? I ask. A bit, he says, only a second. He talks like a telegram, as if he's trying to limit the use of his vocal cords. I shut my eyes, and a sharp pain darts through my body, but I don't make a sound. Done, he says. If you notice blood or fever, call Dr Lauritzen. No hospitals. Don't mention my name.

Sitting in the streetcar on the way home, I'm afraid for the first time. Why is it so secretive and complicated? Why didn't he just take it out? My insides are as quiet as a cathedral; there's no sign that a deadly instrument has just penetrated the membrane which was supposed to protect what wants to live against my will. When I get home Ebbe is sitting there, feeding Helle. He's pale and nervous. I tell him what happened. You shouldn't have done that, he says repeatedly. You're putting your life in danger and that's wrong. We lie awake most of the night. There's no sign of blood or water, no fever, and no one has told me what to expect. Then the air-raid siren sounds. We carry Helle down to the cellar in her bed; this never wakes her up. People are sitting there, half asleep. I talk to the woman who lives downstairs; she's stuffing the mouth of her sleepy, cranky child with cookies. She's young, with a weak, immature face. Maybe she tried to have an abortion too, with that child, or a later one. Maybe lots of women have done what I'm doing now, but no one talks about it. I haven't even told Ebbe the name of the doctor in Charlottenlund, because I don't want him to get in trouble if something happens to me. He helped me as my last resort, and I feel a solidarity with him, even though he was an unpleasant man.

I get cold sitting down here, and I button my fustian jacket up to my neck. I'm so cold my teeth start chattering. I think I might have a fever, I say to Ebbe. The air-raid siren stops, and we go back up to the apartment. I take my temperature, which reads 40°C. Ebbe is beside himself. Call the doctor, he says vehemently. You have to go to the hospital right away. The fever makes me feel like I'm tipsy. Not now, I laugh, it's the middle of the night. Then his wife and children will find out. The last thing I see before falling asleep is Ebbe pacing the floor, furiously running his fingers through his hair. I can't believe this, he mumbles in despair, I can't believe this. Meanwhile I'm thinking: your buddy in the resistance, Hjalmar, he puts your life in danger too, you know.

Early the next morning I call Dr Lauritzen to tell him my fever is 40.5°, but there's no blood or water. It'll come, he promises. Go to the clinic right away; I'll call and tell them you're on your way. But not a word to the nurses, okay? You're pregnant, you have a fever, that's all. And don't be scared. It'll all work out.

It's a nice clinic on Christian IX Gade. The head nurse receives me – a nice, motherly older woman. We might not be able to save the baby, she says, but we'll do what we can. Her words make me wonder, and when I'm shown to a double room, I prop myself up on my elbow and look at the woman in the other bed, who is five or six years older than me and has a sweet, trusting face above the white shirt she's wearing. Her name is Tutti, and to my surprise, she's Morten Nielsen's girlfriend. He's the father of the baby she was going to have. Tutti's divorced, an architect, and she has a six-year-old daughter. Within an hour it's like we've known each other our whole lives. A little Christmas tree stands in the middle of our room with tinkling glass decorations and a star on top. It seems ludicrous, given the circumstances. When I was a child, I say to Tutti in my fevered reverie, I thought that stars really had five points on them. The light goes on, and a nurse arrives with two trays for us. I still can't take the sight or smell of food, so I don't touch it. The nurse asks, are you bleeding? No, I say. Then she leaves a pail and some pads, in case it starts during the night. Dear God, I think in desperation, just let me bleed one drop of blood. After they take away the trays, Ebbe arrives, and then Morten. Hi there, he says, surprised. What are you doing here? Then he sits down on Tutti's bed and they disappear, whispering and embracing. Ebbe has brought me twenty quinine pills which he got from Nadja. Only take them if you have to, he says. After he leaves, I tell Tutti that Nadja once forced a miscarriage by taking quinine. She doesn't see any reason not to take them, so I do it. The night nurse comes in, turns off the ceiling light and turns on the nightlight. Its blue glow illuminates the room with an unreal, ghostly hue. I can't fall asleep, but when I say something to Tutti, I'm unable to hear my own voice. Tutti, I yell, I'm deaf! I can see Tutti moving her lips, but I can't hear anything. Say it louder, I tell her. Then she shouts, You don't have to yell; I'm not deaf. It's those pills, but I think it's just temporary.

There's whooshing in my ears, and behind the whoosh there is a cottony, charged silence. Maybe I've become permanently deaf, for no reason, because there's still no blood. Tutti gets out of bed and walks over to me and shouts in my ear, They just want to see blood. So I'll give you my used pads, and you just show it to them tomorrow morning. Then they'll scrape you out. Talk louder, I say, and finally I'm able to understand what she said. During the night she walks over and places her used pads in my pail. When she passes the Christmas tree, the glass decorations clink together and I know they're tinkling, but I can't hear them. I think about Ebbe and Morten and their desolate expressions amid this woman's world of blood, nausea and fever. And I think of my childhood Christmases, when we walked around the tree singing: Out of the depths we come – instead of singing psalms. I think about my mother. She has no idea I'm lying here, because she can never keep a secret. I also think about my father who has always been hard of hearing, because it runs in his family. Deaf people must live stifled, isolated lives. I might need a hearing aid. But my deafness doesn't mean much next to Tutti's act of mercy. She shouts in my ear, They know full well what's going on here. They just have to keep up appearances.

Towards morning I fall asleep, exhausted, until the nurse comes in and wakes us. My oh my, you've been bleeding a lot, she says with fake worry, looking down into the pail with the night's harvest. I'm afraid we won't be able to save the baby. I'll call the doctor right away. To my relief, I realize that my hearing has come back. Are you sad? asks the nurse. A little, I lie, trying to put on a downcast face.

In the afternoon the doctor comes in, and I'm wheeled to the operating room. Don't feel so bad, he says cheerfully. At least you have one child already. Then they place a mask over my face and the world fills with the smell of ether.

When I wake up, I'm lying in bed with a clean, white shirt on. Tutti smiles over at me. Well, she says, are you happy now? Yes, I say. I don't know what I would have done without you. She doesn't know either, and she says that it's all behind us now. She says Morten wants to marry her. She's madly in love with him and she adores his poetry, which has just been published and has been praised everywhere in the press. Besides you, she says tactfully, he's the most talented young person today. I think so too, but I've never been close to him. Ebbe arrives with flowers like I've just given birth, and he's so happy, because now it's over. We have to be more careful in the future, he says. I go and ask Dr Lauritzen to show me how to put my diaphragm in correctly. Still I harbor a strong resistance to that piece of hardware, a resistance that will remain with me my whole life. My temperature drops quickly to normal, and I'm ravenously hungry now that my nausea has disappeared, as if by a stroke of magic. I miss Helle's little pudgy body with the dimples on her knees. When Ebbe brings her in to me, I think with horror, what if it were her that we had just denied access to life? I bring her up into the bed with me and play with her. She is more dear to me than ever.

In the evening the doctor comes into our room without his coat on, holding two children by the hand. They are ten or twelve years old. Merry Christmas, he says jovially, and squeezes our hands. The children shake hands with us too, and when they're gone, Tutti says: He's so nice. We should be thankful that someone dares to do this.

On Christmas Eve I wake up, take out a pencil and paper from my bag and write a poem in the weak glow of the nightlight:

> You who sought shelter
> with one weak and afraid,
> For you I hum a lullaby
> between the night and day – – –

I don't regret what I did, but in the dark, tarnished corridors of my mind there is a faint impression, like a child's footprints in damp sand.

II

The days pass, the weeks pass, the months pass. I've started writing short stories, and the veil between myself and reality is solid and secure again. Ebbe has started going to hear lectures, and now I'm not so anxious when he's out with Hjalmar. To my relief, he's not as interested in my writing as he once was, so I can create my male characters in peace. But after the episode with Mulvad I'm still careful not to include any obvious similarities to Ebbe. After Helle is in bed in the evening, he reads poems to me from Sophus Claussen or Rilke. Rilke makes a deep impression on me, and I would never have discovered him if it weren't for Ebbe. He's also very interested in Viggo Hørup at the moment. Ebbe poses dramatically with his foot up on a stool and his hand on his heart: My hand, he recites in a deep voice, will always be lifted against the politics that I deem the meanest of all – that which attempts to band together the wealthy and set the upper classes against those who have little to prevent them from being crushed into the dust. In the evening when we are lying in one another's arms, he tells me about his childhood, which is just like every other man's. There is always something about a garden with some fruit trees, and a slingshot, and a cousin or girlfriend they're lying with in a hayloft – but then a mother or aunt comes and ruins it. It's a boring story after you've heard it a few times, but they're so captivated while they tell it. And anyway, what we say to one another doesn't matter all that much, as long as things are good between us.

We've moved to a new apartment on the first floor of the building where Lise and Ole live. It has two and a half rooms, and there's a little yard out front, where Helle can run and play. She's two now, and a cascade of blonde curls has suddenly replaced her baldness. She's so easy that Lise says we don't really know what it's like to raise a child. When I'm writing in the morning, I set her to playing with her blocks and dolls, and she has learned not to bother me. Mama's writing, she says ceremoniously to her doll, and afterwards we will all go for a walk.

She's already speaking in complete sentences. A couple of days before we were going to move into the new apartment, Mrs Hansen called to me from the kitchen. The HIPOs* have blocked the street, she says. Look over there, there's a bonfire. I pull aside the curtain and look down. Across the deserted street HIPOs are tossing pieces of furniture out of the top window of the building facing ours, and burning them in a big bonfire. Down below there's a woman with her hands up, standing against the building wall with two children. Men shouting commands are holding them there with their machine guns. Mrs Hansen says, Those poor people – but luckily this damned war will soon be over.

Just as I'm about to leave my lookout, a woman comes

* The Hilfspolizei, a Gestapo-backed pseudo-police force of Danish citizens that patrolled and terrorized Copenhagen in 1944.

running at full speed around the corner and I see, to my horror, that it's Tutti. A HIPO man shouts at her and shoots into the sky, and she disappears into our entry. When I let her in, she falls on me sobbing: Morten is dead, she says, and at first the words don't quite register. I get her to sit down, and I can see that she's wearing two different shoes. Dead how? I ask. Is it true? I just saw him two days ago. Tutti tells me between sobs that it was a stray bullet, an accident, completely meaningless, and unbearable. He was sitting across from an officer who was going to show him how to use a pistol with a silencer. Suddenly the gun went off and hit Morten right in the heart. He was only twenty-two, says Tutti, looking at me desperately. I loved him so much. I don't think I'll ever get over this.

I can see Morten's angular honest face before me, and I remember his poem: I have known death since I was a boy. It's so strange, I say, how he wrote so much about death. I know, says Tutti, calming down a little. It was as if he knew that he wouldn't be allowed to live.

Later that day, Ester and Halfdan come by, and they're both shocked. I know that Halfdan was very close with Morten. But what I can't get out of my mind is that the same thing could happen to Ebbe. Now it feels gravely serious when he goes out to meet Hjalmar, and I feel anxious until I see him again. We move into the new apartment and we visit Lise and Ole during curfew. After a tuberculosis exam, which all students have to go through once a year, Ole is told that he has 'something in his chest'. If it weren't for that, he says, he would train to join the resistance too. The doctor decided that Ole has to live for a few months at a college in Holte for students with tuberculosis, and Lise isn't too upset about their separation. Now she can put off their divorce and see her lawyer in peace.

Then arrives the fifth of May, Liberation Day, with jubilant crowds cheering in the streets, as if they've sprouted up from between the paving stones. Strangers embrace one another, bawl out the freedom song and cheer hurray every time a car carrying resistance fighters drives past. Ebbe is in full uniform, and I'm worried what will happen to him, because no one knows if the Germans will pull back without a fight. Upstairs, at Lise and Ole's, the pullimut bottles are on the table for the last time, and there are lots of people there, and we don't know them all. We dance, celebrate and enjoy ourselves, but this historic event doesn't really penetrate my consciousness, because I always experience things after they've happened; I'm rarely in the present. We tear down the blackout curtains and stomp them to pieces. We're acting like we're happy, but really we're not. Tutti is still grieving for Morten; Lise and Ole are separating; and Sinne has just left Arne, who is so depressed that he doesn't get out of bed. Nadja, who is always hunting for a man, but always the wrong one, is trying to get together with Ebbe's brother Karsten, who she would fit like a ring in his nose. Meanwhile I'm thinking about my abortion and I'm always calculating how old the baby would have been by now. Something has gone wrong for each one of us, and I think that our youth has disappeared along with the occupation. Helle and Kim are sleeping in the nursery, and when they cry so loud that we can hear it over our own noise, Lise goes in and sings them back to sleep. Outside in the sky, the spring night revolves and the elegantly suspended moon observes a drunken and dead-tired crowd, who can't bear to leave and go home.

A couple of days later, Ebbe comes home pale and agitated. He tells me how the traitors and collaborators are being treated at Dagmarhus, the previous Gestapo headquarters.

He takes off his uniform and puts on his civilian clothes. When I take a walk with Helle at Vesterbro Square, I see a group of unarmed German soldiers come shuffling, out of step and with exhausted, hopeless faces. They are quite young, some of them only fifteen or sixteen. When I get home I write a poem about them. It starts:

> Tired German soldiers
> trudging in a strange city,
> not looking at one another,
> spring light on their foreheads.
> Tired, hesitating, shy,
> in the middle of a strange city
> they approach defeat.

One day Lise comes down to visit us and tells me that Ole is inviting a lot of young women to a 'Tubercular Ball' which they are holding at the Rudershøj dormitory. Ebbe is upset that he can't go, but there are already more than enough men, so it's no use. I'm happy to be invited, because my short-story collection is finished, and I don't know what to do with myself when I'm not writing. Lise says that the dean's wife's son will be there to lure his mother to bed early.

When we get there, the party is in full force. People are dancing to a local band, and none of the students look any worse than Ole, who is the picture of health. A big-chested woman comes rushing up to welcome us. She is evidently the dean's wife. I dance with lots of different men in a large, open room with a parquet floor and high-backed chairs along the walls. The dormitory is located in a large park, which is veiled that evening by a rainy haze, greenish, black and silvery under a misty moon, sailing between the clouds. A bar has been set up in a kind of foyer, with a counter and high chairs and a bartender who is pouring real liquor and not pullimut. For some reason I feel happy and free, and I have a feeling that something special is going to happen before the night is over. I'm drinking whiskey, and I get drunk, jolly and impetuous. On one of the barstools, Sinne is sitting on a young man's lap. I sit next to them and say traitorously, You're betting on the wrong horse; she's engaged to a black marketeer. The young man brushes Sinne off as if she were a fleck of dust. I never thought, he says to me, that poets could be so beautiful. Then, from the shade of the lamp, his face emerges, and I find myself observing it with the attention of a painter of miniatures. He has thinning reddish hair, relaxed gray eyes, and teeth so crooked it looks like they are in two rows. It turns out he is the dean's wife's son, and has completed his medical degree. I'm surprised to meet a student who has actually finished. He dances with me, and we trip over one another's feet and have to give up, laughing. Then we take a walk in the park. The night is clearing and the air is like damp silk. He kisses me beneath a silver-gray birch tree, then suddenly his mother comes rushing out to us with her undulating violet silk bust and waving arms. Young people nowadays, she pants. The contents of her mind are expressed primarily in half-intelligible sentimental outbursts. Then her son, whose name is Carl, remembers his promise to the students to take his mother home to bed, and he mutters something to me about us getting together later, and he disappears into the building with her.

Then the party gets wilder. People are dancing, drinking and carrying on. Pair after pair disappear up the stairs and don't reappear. I'm more drunk than I have been in a long time, and when Carl returns he suggests that we go up to his room so he can get some sleep. I think that sounds like a fine idea. I've forgotten about Ebbe, and about my promise to be faithful to him.

In the morning I wake up with a horrible headache. I glance at the man sleeping next to me and realize that he is quite ugly with all those teeth and that underbite which doesn't hide them. I wake him and say that I'm going home. I'm irritated and sluggish, and I put on my clothes without a word. I decide I never want to see him again, and when he asks if he can walk me home, I say, No thanks, I would rather go alone. When I go down to the messy ballroom, I sit down for a moment on one of the bar chairs. Down the stairs comes Sinne on the heels of a very tall young man, who is holding her bra in one hand. Without taking the least notice of him she walks over to me and asks, Dear God, what did we drink? He was hideous, over six feet tall, and probably only had half a lung. Then she grabs the bra and disappears with a sleepy yawn.

I leave the battlefield and bicycle home to Ebbe, who is furious that I stayed out all night. You probably slept with someone else, he says. I plead my innocence, but actually find it humorous that it should matter so much. There are other forms of loyalty that mean so much more. When I go to bed, I realize that I didn't have my diaphragm in. Otherwise I have always been so careful since my abortion. Then I think that if something does happen, at least he's a doctor, so that should make it easier than last time.

12

Good God, I say. He has an underbite and sixty-four teeth in his mouth instead of thirty-two. And I don't know if it's his or Ebbe's. Lise, what should I do?

I pace the floor, and Lise watches me with two deep furrows on her forehead. You get pregnant just walking through a draft, she says with a sigh. But if he's a doctor he should be able to get rid of it without all the trouble you went through last time. But do I have to see him again? I say. He's so hideous, and what do I tell Ebbe? Things have never been as good between us as they are now. Lise explains to me patiently that I have to see him again. I have to call his mother and find out where he lives. And I can tell Ebbe anything – that I'm going over to visit Nadja or Ester, or that I'm going to visit my parents; he's not suspicious. So we have coffee, and Lise tells me that she's not doing so well either. Her lawyer won't get a divorce after all, but he still wants to be with her. Isn't it terrible, she says, these men with two women. Both of them are suffering, and the man won't choose. She brushes her short brown hair away from her cheek and looks miserable, and it makes me feel bad that I'm always dumping my own problems on her. If I'm not writing, I say, then I'm pregnant. That makes us laugh, and we agree that I have to do something. I'll have to get Carl's address and visit him and have him get rid of it.

The next day Carl calls me himself and asks if we can get together soon. I say yes, and I agree to come and visit him the following evening. He lives at the Biochemical Institute, where he also works. He's a scientist. I tell Ebbe that I'm going to visit Nadja, and I ride my bicycle through the twilight down Nørre Allé, where the trees are as motionless as a drawing. It's summer, and I'm wearing a white cotton dress that I bought from Sinne. Carl's room looks like any student's dorm: a bed, a table, a couple of chairs and some shelves full of books. He's bought sandwiches, beer and schnapps, but I don't touch any of it. We sit at the table and I say: I'm pregnant, and I don't want to have a child when I don't know who the father is. I see, he says, relaxed, looking at me with his serious gray eyes, which are the only pleasant thing about him. I can help you with that. Come tomorrow evening and I can do a curettage. He says this as if it's something he does every day, and he seems like the kind of person that nothing in the world could bother. I smile, relieved, and say: Can you give me anesthesia? I'll give you a shot, he says, so you won't feel a thing. A shot? I ask. What is it? Morphine or Demerol, he says. Demerol is the best. Morphine makes a lot of people throw up. So I calm down, and I eat and drink with him after all. I'm only eight days late, and my morning sickness hasn't started yet. Carl has small, thin, quick hands, which remind me a little of Viggo F.'s. He has a nice voice and he's well spoken. He tells me he went to boarding school at Herlufsholm, that his mother got a divorce when he was two, and that as far back as he can remember, he always wanted her to remarry.

He also tells me that his father, as far as he knows, is in a home for alcoholics, but that he's had no contact with him since he left them. He also tells me that, since we met, he's been reading everything I've written; and he adds, smiling, that we could have a fine child together. He would like to marry me. I already have a very suitable husband, I say, and a lovely daughter, so that will have to wait. Okay, he says, rubbing his chin as if he were checking for stubble. It probably wouldn't be such a great idea to marry me anyway, he says. I have to tell you that I am a little crazy. He says this in complete seriousness, and I ask what he could possibly mean by that. But he can't really explain it. It's just a feeling he has. He says there's a lot of mental illness on his father's side, and also that his mother isn't too bright. I laugh and don't give it another thought. When I'm leaving, he gives me a gentle kiss, but doesn't try to get me to go to bed with him. I think I'm in love with you, he says, but it's probably no use.

When I come home, Ebbe is reading poetry by Thøger Larsen while puffing on his pipe, which he has started doing after reading that cigarettes can cause cancer. He doesn't want Helle and me to lose him to an early death. He asks how Nadja is doing, and I tell him the truth – that she's gotten engaged to a student from the University of Copenhagen, and that she spouts the most reactionary opinions, as if she were from before the reign of Frederik VI. He chuckles and says that she should get married and have children. We're getting old, he says, tapping out his pipe in the ashtray. He is twenty-seven and I'm twenty-five. When I think about my childhood, he says, I feel just like Thøger Larsen. Listen to this:

> Be glad if you meet a withered glimpse
> in dreams from the spring of your youth.

A ray of grace. Your father is near.
Your mother is in the kitchen.

My mother, I object, is over fifty, and I don't think she's old at all. My mother is sixty-five, he says, and I've never thought she was young. It makes a difference. I don't really follow him when he talks about how old he is, and everything I have to hide from him is also creating distance between us. When we go to bed, I say that I'm exhausted and that I have to go straight to sleep. Tomorrow, I say, I want to visit Ester and Halfdan. When he says he'd like to come, I say that we can't always have Lise watching Helle, and his mother doesn't really like watching her either. But I promise him not to stay too long.

The next evening, while I'm sitting in a streetcar on the way to Carl's, I tell myself that it's not definite that I'm pregnant. It could be just a fluctuation in my period; that's not so uncommon. I say this because I don't want another shadow to crop up next to Helle, another one whose age I will always have to calculate. I know that some women get scraped out just to clean their inner parts. When I arrive, I see that Carl has obtained a high table for the occasion. It stands in the center of the room, and there's a white sheet over it. He has also put his pillow on it, so I can be comfortable. He's wearing a white lab coat, and he washes his hands and scrubs his nails, while he pleasantly asks me to make myself comfortable. There are some shiny instruments on the bookshelf next to the table. When he's washed his hands, he takes a syringe from the glass shelf over the sink. He fills it with a clear liquid and lays it next to the instruments; then he ties a rubber hose around my upper arm. You'll feel a little prick, he says calmly. You'll hardly feel it. He taps lightly on the inner side of my elbow, until a blue blood vessel protrudes. You have good veins, he says. Then he gives me the injection, and a bliss I have never before felt spreads through my entire body. The room expands to a radiant hall, and I feel completely relaxed, lazy and happy as never before. I roll over on my side and close my eyes. Leave me alone, I hear myself say, as if through many layers of cotton. You don't have to do anything to me.

When I wake up, Carl is standing there washing his hands again. I still have the blissful feeling, and I have the sense that it will disappear if I move. You can get up and put your clothes on, he says, drying his hands. It's done. I do what he says, slowly, without telling him how happy I feel. He asks if I want a beer, but I shake my head. He says I need some fluids, and he takes out a soda which I force myself to drink. He sits down on the bed next to me and kisses me carefully. Was it painful? he asks. No, I say. What was it you gave me? I ask. Demerol, he says, a painkiller. I take his hand and put it up to my cheek. I'm in love with you, I say. I'll come back soon. He looks happy, and in that moment I think he is almost handsome. He has a solid, durable face, made to last his whole life. Ebbe's face is fragile, scarred in many places, and might be used up by the time he's forty. It's a strange thought, and I don't know how to express it. When I come back, I say slowly, can I have another shot of that? He laughs and rubs his protruding chin. Sure, he says, if you think it's so wonderful. You don't have the makings of an addict. I wish I could marry you, I say, stroking his soft, thin hair. What about your husband? he says. I'll just move out, I say, and take Helle with me. While I ride home in the streetcar, the effects of the shot wear off slowly, and it feels as if a gray, slimy veil covers whatever my eyes see. Demerol, I think. The name sounds like birdsong. I decide never to let go of this man who can give me such an indescribable blissful feeling.

When I get home, Ebbe wants to know how Ester and Halfdan were, but I only give him one-word answers. When he asks me what's wrong, I tell him I have a toothache. I roll over on my side in bed, with my back to him, touching the little bump on my elbow from the injection. I am preoccupied with the single thought of doing it again. I could not care less about Ebbe or anyone else but Carl.

PART TWO

I

Ebbe has since died, but whenever I try to recall his face, I always see him the way he looked that day I told him there was someone else. We were sitting at the table, eating with Helle. He put down his knife and fork and pushed back his plate. He was pale, and a nerve in his cheek was vibrating slightly, but that was the only sign of any disturbance. Then he got up from his chair, walked over to the bookshelf, took out his pipe and carefully started filling it. Then he paced the floor, puffing violently on the pipe while staring at the ceiling, as if he could find an answer up there. Do you want a divorce? he asked in a flat, calm voice. I don't know, I said. For the meantime Helle and I can move out for a while. Maybe we'll come back. Suddenly he put down his pipe and picked up Helle in his arms, which he rarely did. Daddy sad, she said, putting her cheek against his. No, he said, forcing himself to smile, go on and finish eating. He put her back down in her high chair, picked up his pipe again, and resumed pacing. Then he said: I don't understand why people absolutely have to get married or live together. It forces you to see the same person every day for a generation, and there's something unnatural about that. Maybe things would be better if we only visited one another. Who's the other man? he asked, without looking at me. He's a doctor, I said. I met him at the Tubercular Ball. He sat down again, and I saw how his forehead was bathed in sweat. Then he said, still looking at the ceiling: Do you think he can give you an outlook on life? When Ebbe was upset, he always said stupid things. I don't know what you mean by that, I said. I don't think an outlook on life is something people give one another.

When we went to bed, Ebbe held me in his arms for the last time, but he could tell I was distant and distracted. Right, he said. You're in love with someone else. This is something that happens to people, not even unusual in our circles. Still it feels totally unreal. And it's crushing me, even though I'm not showing it. That's one of my problems, that I don't dare to show how I feel. If I had shown you how much I love you, maybe this would never have happened. Ebbe, I said, gently touching his eyelids, we'll visit each other, and maybe you'll get to know Carl. Maybe we can all be friends. No, he said with a sudden vehemence, I never want to lay eyes on that man. I only want to see you and Helle. I propped myself up on my elbow and observed his handsome face with its soft, weak expression. What if I told him the truth? What if I told him I was in love with a clear liquid in a syringe and not with the man who had the syringe? But I didn't tell him; I never told that to anyone. It was like when I was a small child and a secret was ruined if you told a grownup. I rolled over on my side and went to sleep. The next day Helle and I moved to a boarding house that Carl had found for us.

It was a boarding house for older, single women. Our room was furnished with cretonne-covered wicker furniture, a rocking chair with a pillow attached to the back, a tall iron bed from the 1880s and a small feminine writing desk, which nearly collapsed when I set my heavy typewriter on it. Even Helle's little crib seemed too robust in these fragile surroundings, not to mention herself. That first day she played ship with the overturned rocking chair and then she started chewing on a horribly ugly life-sized statue of Christ, which was behind the desk. She was craving calcium at the time. Her piercing child's voice rang through the convent-like hush with a provocative intensity, and one by one the old ladies turned up at my door, asking for a bit of quiet. I don't know why I ever was allowed to move in. When I started writing on my typewriter the next day, the whole boarding house was in an uproar, and the manager, who was an old lady herself, came in to ask if all that racket was really necessary. The residents in her boarding house were all people who had retreated from life, she said. Even their families considered them dead. At any rate no one ever visited them; their families were just waiting to inherit whatever bit of money they might have left. I paid attention to what she said, because I wanted to stay. I liked the location and the room, and the view of the two maple trees, between which hung an old ragged hammock whose rope weave was still covered with snow, though it was nearly March. The woman had a sickly, mild face with pretty, gentle eyes, and she picked Helle up and carefully put her on her lap, as if the vibrant girl might break from the least handling. I agreed not to use the typewriter between one and three in the afternoon, when the ladies were resting, and I promised to visit them once in a while, since their families had deserted them. I liked being with the ladies who either were not completely deaf, or whose fate in this end-station had not made them angry and bitter. And there was always one of them who could watch Helle while I saw Carl in the evenings, which I often did. I sat on his ottoman with my arms under my chin and my knees pulled up, watching him while he worked. He had lots of flasks and beakers in wooden stands around the room. He tasted the contents of the beakers and slid his tongue thoughtfully between his lips. Then he wrote his observations in a large notebook. I asked what he was testing. Piss, he said calmly. Yuck, I said. Then he smiled and said, There is nothing as sterile as piss. He had a strange, careful way of walking, as if he were trying to avoid waking someone, and the desk lamp imparted a copper-like glow to his thin hair. The first three times I visited him he gave me a shot every time and let me lie there passively, dreaming away, without bothering me. But the fourth time he said, No; we'd better take a break. It's not candy, you know. I was so disappointed I got tears in my eyes.

When Ebbe visited me and Helle, he was almost always drunk, and his face was so blank and defenseless that I couldn't bear to look at him. While I sat looking at the two maple trees, with whose branches the sun and wind drew shifting patterns of shadow on the lawn, I thought that I was not a woman whom any man ought to marry. Ebbe played with Helle a little, and she said: Daddy is nice. Helle doesn't like Carl. It took a long time before she would let Carl touch her.

I had delivered a short-story collection and lost my desire to write for the time being. All I could think about was how to get Carl to give me another shot of Demerol. I remembered that he had said it was a painkiller. Where could I say it hurt? From an old untreated infection, one of my ears oozed once in a while, so one day when I was lying on his bed while he tiptoed around the room, chatting intermittently with me and with himself, I put my hand on my ear and said, Ow, I have a terrible earache. He came and sat next to me on the bed and asked sympathetically: Does it hurt badly? I grimaced as if I were in pain. Yes, I said, I can't stand it. I get this once in a while. He moved the lamp so he could look inside my ear. It's oozing, he said, surprised. Promise me you'll have an ear doctor look at it. He patted my cheek. Relax, he said. I'll give you a shot. I smiled thankfully at him, and the fluid went into my blood, lifting me up to the only level where I wanted to exist. Then he went to bed with me, like he always did, when the effect was at its peak. His embrace was strangely brief and violent, with no foreplay, no tenderness; and I didn't feel anything. Light, gentle, untroubled thoughts glided through my head. I thought warmly about all my friends who I almost never saw anymore, and I fantasized that I was having conversations with them. How is it possible, Lise said to me recently, that you could be in love with him? I said, Who can ever understand someone else's love? I lay there for a couple of hours, and the effect wore off, so it was more difficult to find that blank, untroubled state. Everything returned to being gray, slimy, ugly and intolerable. When I said goodbye, Carl asked when my divorce would be finalized. Anytime, I said, figuring that once I was married to him it would be even easier to get him to give me shots. Wouldn't you like to have another baby? he asked as he walked me out, down the stairs. Sure, I said immediately, because a child would bind Carl to me even more, and I wanted him with me for the rest of my life.

2

In the divorce I was given our apartment, which I moved into together with Helle and Carl. Ebbe moved back in with his mother, and I visited him there sometimes, when he called and asked me to come. He never set foot in our apartment again, for fear of running into Carl. But Lise and Ole visited us, as did Arne and Sinne, who were back together, since her black marketeer was doing time. Back when I was with Ebbe, I thought it was so friendly with all of us visiting one another unannounced, but now it really irritated me. It bothered Carl too, because he was jealous of all my friends. Whenever they came over to visit, he would sit with his shy, quiet smile, rarely saying a word. One day Lise asked me cautiously, Isn't he a little strange? I replied brusquely that he worked hard during the day and he was tired in the evening. And what about you? she asked. You've changed since you met him; you've lost weight, and you don't look so healthy anymore. Listen, I said to her angrily, you never like anyone except the students from Høng, and you think anyone who's not chatty and extroverted is strange. She was so hurt by what I said that she stayed away from me for a long time.

One evening shortly after Carl and I had gotten married, Arne and Sinne invited us over for a big dinner. Sinne had had half a pig sent from her family's farm, and they were going to have a party. Carl said he wasn't going to go, and that he thought I should stay home too. When a person has work that requires concentration, he said, with that apologetic tone that never revealed his true intention, it's not good to be overloaded with human interactions. These are my friends, I protested. I see no reason why I shouldn't go to the dinner. Will you stay home, he said gently, if I give you a shot? Bowled over, and for the first time a little frightened, I said, Sure, sure I will. The next morning I felt so miserable that I couldn't even get up and make coffee for him. The light seared my eyes, and I could barely separate my dry, cracked lips. It felt as if my skin couldn't bear the pressure of the sheet and the blanket. Everything I cast my eyes on was ugly, hard and sharp. I pushed Helle away from me and snapped at her, which made her cry. What's wrong, asked Carl. Is it your ear again? Yes, I whined, putting my hand to my ear. Dear God, I thought in desperation, please let him believe me just one last time. Don't let him leave for work before giving me a shot. Let me see it, he said gently, and he took an ear speculum and a little flashlight down from the top shelf in the closet, where he kept the instruments from the curettage. It looks pretty good, he mumbled, and since you're going to the ear doctor twice a week, it should be under control. While he looked in my ear, I lay there without blinking to get my eyes to tear up. I'm rather worried, he said, filling the syringe. If this keeps up, there might be no way around an operation. I'll speak with Falbe Hansen about it. He was the ear doctor Carl had found for me. Why are you giving Mama a needle? asked Helle, who had never seen this before. I'm giving her a vaccine against diphtheria, he said, just like you had. It's supposed to be in your shoulder, she said. Why are you putting it in her arm? That's the way you do it with grownups, he said. Limp and distant and peaceful I watched while Carl drank his coffee and spooned out Helle's oatmeal for her. Lazy and blissful I said goodbye to Carl, but far back in my foggy brain anxiety began gnawing. Operation! There was nothing wrong with my ear. Then I forgot about it again and lay there fantasizing about a novel I was going to write. It was going to be called *For the Sake of the Child*, and I was writing it in my mind. Long, beautiful sentences flowed through my thoughts as I lay on the divan, looking at my typewriter, powerless to make one single movement towards it. Helle crawled around on me and had to dress herself. I said that she should go upstairs and get Kim, so they could play together outside in the yard. When the effect of the shot wore off, I broke out in sobs and pulled the comforter up to my chin because I was shivering, even though it was the start of summer. This is awful, I said out into the air, I can't take this. What am I going to do? So I got dressed, with difficulty, because my hands were shaking, and every piece of clothing scratched my skin. I thought of calling Carl, so he could come home and give me another shot. The hours in front of me seemed like years, and I didn't think I could survive them. Then I got a bad stomachache and I had to go to the toilet. I had gotten diarrhea and I had to run out there every five minutes.

Later in the day I felt a bit better. I even sat in front of my typewriter and started that novel which had been haunting my thoughts for a long time. But the words didn't come easy and flowing like they usually did, and I had trouble keeping my thoughts on the subject. I kept looking at my watch to see how long it would be until Carl came home.

Around noon, John came over to visit. He was a friend of Carl's, a tubercular medical student who was living at Rudershøj with my mother-in-law. I didn't like him, because whenever he visited us, he tended to sit in a corner and stare at me with his big X-ray eyes, as if I represented a difficult problem that he had to solve at all costs. He and Carl usually talked over my head about incomprehensible scientific questions, and I had never been alone with him before. I'd like to talk to you, he said solemnly, if you have a moment. I let him come in, while my heart started thumping with a strange, indefinite fear. John sat on my desk chair, while I sat on the ottoman. When he sat down, he gave the impression of being tall, because his face was large and squarish, his shoulders broad and his body long and stooped. But he had short legs and they didn't get much longer when he stood up. He and Carl had lived together at Regensen, and they had helped one another write their theses. He sat quietly for a while, wringing his big hands as if he were cold. I looked down at the floor, because I couldn't stand his penetrating stare. Then he said, I'm worried about Carl, and maybe about you too. Why? I said, on guard. We're doing fine together. He bent over to catch my gaze, and I looked at him, obstinate and afraid. Has Carl ever told you, he said, about his institutionalization a year ago? Ill at ease, I said, What kind of institutionalization? In a psychiatric ward, he said; he had a psychosis. Why can't you talk Danish, I said, irritated. What's a psychosis? It's a short-lived mental illness, he said, leaning back in the chair. It lasted three months. I forced myself to laugh. I said, Are you telling me that he's crazy? Crazy people get locked up, because they're scary. I'm not scared of him. John released me from his unnerving gaze, and he looked out in the yard at the children playing. There's something wrong, he said.

I have a feeling he's getting sick again. When I asked why, John said that Carl had recently ignored all his work in order to study nothing but ear maladies. At the institute there were textbooks piling up about ear anatomy and ear illnesses, and he was studying them as if he were trying to become an ear doctor. That's crazy, said John emphatically. Just because you have a little earache once in a while? Anyone else would leave it to an ear doctor and trust that he would do what he could. But he cares about me, I said, and I could feel myself blushing. He cares about me, and he wants to help me get better, that's all. Then I laughed at his serious mortician's face. Some friend you are, I said, running over to tell his wife that he's stark raving mad. I'm not saying that at all, he said irresolutely. I just want you to know that three of his cousins are in a mental institution. I wouldn't recommend having any children with him. When he says that, I realize that my period is a few days late. Well you know what, I say, I think your warning has come too late; I think I might be pregnant. The thought of it makes me happy, and I ask if John wants a beer or a cup of coffee, because I don't feel like listening to him anymore. But he doesn't want anything; he's going to a lecture. I follow him out to the door, and he sticks out his hand to shake mine, something my friends and I never do. I'm being admitted to Avnstrup in a few days, he says, to have one of my lungs taken out of action. For a person like me, health is not something you take for granted. He hesitates a second more before he leaves. And you, he says, just like Lise did, you don't look as good as you used to. Are you eating enough? I assure him that I am, and I breathe easy again once he's finally gone. I decide, even though he didn't ask me to, not to tell Carl that he was here.

When Carl came home, I told him that I was probably

pregnant. He was happy and revealed his plan for us to build a house on the outskirts of the city. I asked if we had enough money for that, and he said that he was expecting a large grant to come through soon. Then we could live in our own house, concentrate on our work, and not see so many people and never go anywhere. I thought that sounded marvelous, because I was starting to feel that it was becoming necessary for us to live without interference from other people. When he asked about my ear, I said that the pain had gone away. John's visit had frightened me. Then I said, without knowing why, that I always had trouble sleeping when I was pregnant. He thought about it, rubbing his chin. I'll tell you what, he said. I'll give you some chloral. It's a good sedative with no side effects. It tastes awful, but you can just drink it in some milk.

The next day he came home with a large brown bottle of medicine. I'd better pour it for you, he said. It's easy to take too much. A few minutes after drinking it I was feeling good, not like after Demerol, more like I had had too much alcohol. I blabbed on about our house, how it would be furnished, and the baby we were going to have. Then in the middle of this I fell asleep and didn't wake up until the next morning. Can I have that every night? I asked. Sure, of course, he said. It can't do any harm. Then he thought of something. Let me feel behind your ear, he said, pressing on my skull. Does that hurt? he asked. Yes, I said. Lying to Carl had become such a habit that I couldn't resist. He bit his top lip pensively. I'm going to talk with Falbe Hansen about that operation after all, he said. I asked if I would be anesthetized with Demerol. He said no, but that afterwards I could have as much as I wanted to numb the pain. After he left, I walked to the bathroom and stared at my face in the mirror for a long time. It was true. I didn't look good. My face was drawn, and my skin was dry and rough. I wonder, I said to my reflection, which of us is crazy. Then I sat down at my typewriter, because that was my one remaining hope in a more and more uncertain world. While I wrote, I thought: all the Demerol I want; and the operation, which would be the prerequisite for entering that paradise, didn't matter to me one bit.

3

But the doctor wouldn't do the operation. After the X-rays were taken, Carl and I rode to his office on the motorcycle he had just bought. He stood next to Falbe Hansen in his leather jacket, which flared out in the back like a duck's ass. And with his helmet in his hand, he stared at the pictures the doctor held up one after the other. There's nothing abnormal, said Falbe Hansen. I walked over and stood next to Carl, and while the ear doctor spoke, he stared at me the whole time with a cool look in his gray eyes. If she's in pain, he said slowly, then it must be from rheumatism, and nothing can be done for that. It usually goes away by itself. Then Carl talked about bones, hammers, anvils, stirrups and God knows what, while I felt the earth burning beneath me, because this man knew I was lying. Falbe Hansen's attitude got even more icy. You won't get anyone to operate on it, he said, sitting down at his desk with a distracted expression. That ear is completely healthy. I have had it dried out, and your wife doesn't need to come back and see me anymore.

Don't worry, Carl said gently while we walked back through the hospital grounds. If the pain keeps up, we'll find someone else to operate. Maybe the conversation did make some kind of impression on him, because when we got home he said: I'll write a prescription for you for some pills called methadone. It's a strong painkiller; then it won't matter if I'm home or not. He wrote the prescription on a piece of my typewriter paper, and then he cut the edges carefully. He admired his work with a smile. He said, It looks kind of fake. If they want to check on it, you can just give them my number at the institute. What do you mean fake? I said. It looks like you wrote it yourself, he chuckled. That's how some real addicts do it. He often used the expression 'real addicts' when making comparisons to me. Then I realized that I thought I saw a real addict once. I told him about the day I was sitting in Abortion-Lauritz's office and a woman was pacing adamantly and begging to go into the office first. Then when she came out, just a few minutes later, she was completely changed, talkative and lively, and with shining eyes. Yes, said Carl, that probably was a real addict. When I was alone I looked more carefully at the prescription and I thought he was right: anyone could have written this. Then I went to the pharmacy and got the pills. When I came home I took them right away to see how they worked; maybe they would take away my nausea. It was a Saturday afternoon. Lise was free early and she came over to pick up Kim, who played with Helle almost every day. Our relationship had cooled since that day when she asked me if Carl was strange, but I asked her to stay for a while, so we could chat, like in the old days. I felt happy and positive and accommodating, and she said she was glad to see I was my old self again. I said, That's because I'm writing. That's the only thing that really works for me. I made us coffee and while we drank it I asked how she was. I was feeling guilty for neglecting her for so long. Not so good, she said. Married men are a load of crap, but I can't get away from him. Ole had had a jealous neurosis, and he went to a psychoanalyst named Sachs Jacobsen who Lise thought was incompetent. Then last Sunday morning Lise had bought nice rolls, since Kim was sick, and Ole made a big stink about it. The next day Sachs Jacobsen called Lise on the phone at work. She was German. Well your husband must doch need his warm buns, she said. We had a good laugh about it, and our old friendship was quietly being restored. I wanted to tell her something private too, so I told her about Carl's obsession with my ear and his plan to get me an operation. That's terrible, she said, visibly horrified. Don't do that, Tove. You can get deaf from an operation like that. That happened to one of my aunts. And you never had an earache before you met Carl. No, I said, but I get them now sometimes. Then I thought about the important letter that Carl had received a few days before. It was from a girl in Skælskør who was informing him that she was going to have a baby of his in a month or so, and that she hadn't written before, because she thought it was a tumor. The baby was going to be given away for adoption in consideration of her very respectable family. Carl had suggested to me that we adopt it, and I had tepidly said yes, since I didn't think one child more or less made any difference. Besides – but this I didn't tell Lise – it would be very difficult for him to leave me if I adopted his child. That sounds like a good idea, said Lise, who, like Nadja, made a habit of saving people, helping them, and relieving them of their burdens. You'll have plenty of room when you move out to your new house. Then I'll do it, I said, as if I were talking about taking a walk in the woods. And Carl has promised me house-help too. I can't write and also take care of three children. Lise thought that sounded sensible. Then you'll have someone to make food for you too, she said, tapping absent-mindedly on her front teeth with her index finger. You need that. Look how thin you've become. Then she fetched Kim from the yard and went back to their place. I went into the bathroom and took two more pills. Then I sat down to write, and for the first time in a long time the words just flowed, just like in the old days, I forgot everything around me, including the reason for my peace of mind, which was inside a bottle in the bathroom.

In October of 1945 we brought home the newborn girl from the National Hospital. She was tiny and only weighed about five pounds. She had red hair and long golden eyelashes. That day I had taken four pills, because they didn't have as strong an effect on me anymore. I thought it was wonderful having a newborn in my arms again, and I promised myself that I would care for her as if she were mine. She needed a bottle every three hours, night and day, and at night Carl got up and fed her. I couldn't wake up from my chloral-sleep. When my mother came to see the new baby, she glanced in the crib and said: Well, you couldn't call her pretty. She thought it was insane that I would take on more children than absolutely necessary. My mother-in-law came to visit too. She just about fainted with emotion. Dear God, she said, putting her hands to her heart, she looks so much like Carl. Then she went on at length about how her cook had left her, and how difficult it was to find another one. She was always having trouble with her cooks. What should I do for my hot flushes? she asked her son, who always had to get tipsy to be able to endure her visits. He smiled. That sounds nice, he said, with this cool summer we're having. He never took her seriously, and when she went to kiss him, he did a little skip to avoid her embrace. Then at the last second he turned his cheek, so she could give him a kiss. Whenever she came over, he had me put on a dress with long sleeves to hide the needle marks on my arms. Not that it matters that much, he said, but it doesn't look so great.

Jabbe was installed in our apartment, and for the moment had to sleep in the kids' room. Her name was Miss Jacobsen and she was from Grenå, but since Helle called her Jabbe, the rest of us did too. She was a large, strong, skilled girl who loved children. She had a simple, reliable face with protruding eyes that were always a bit damp, as if she were constantly moved to tears. She woke up early in the morning to bake rolls for breakfast, which she served me in bed, while Carl slept beside me. You have to eat, she said. You're too thin. My appetite improved a little, now that the food was being served to me, and it seemed that everything was getting better. I worked well on methadone, and I was happy to get a shot just once in a while. Ebbe called me frequently when he was drunk. He wandered the bars with Victor, whom I had never met, although many of my friends knew him. Ebbe really wanted me to meet this Victor. But whenever I said to Carl that I was thinking of going over to visit Ebbe, the syringe came out and he went to bed with me in his coarse, careless way. I love passive women, he said. When he acknowledged that Ebbe had a valid reason to see his daughter, we arranged it so I could drop her off at Ebbe's mother's once in a while, and then she brought her back after the visit.

I gave birth to Michael at a clinic on Enghave Street, and Carl helped bring the child into the world. Afterwards, while I lay in the private room with our infant in my arms, he gave me a shot and sat by my bed for a long time, observing his child, who was immediately put back into the crib. This is going to be an incredible child, he said proudly; the son of an artist and a scientist – a good combination. I'm looking forward to the house being finished, I said sluggishly, while the familiar sweetness flowed into all my extremities. We will always stay together, Carl said with conviction. It won't be like with the others. Viggo F. and Ebbe didn't understand you like I do.

A short while later we moved out to the finished house which was located on Ewaldsbakken in Gentofte. It was a completely custom-built brick house with two stories. On the ground floor was the children's room, the maid's room, the dining room, the bathroom and the kitchen. Upstairs, Carl and I each had our own room. Mine was large and bright, and from my desk I could see down into the beautiful yard with many fruit trees in the lawn, which Carl mowed every Sunday morning. That summer was relatively happy. We had created a civilized frame around our life, a dream that I had always harbored deep down. Whatever I earned I gave to Carl, who managed our finances skillfully and economically as far as I could tell. But one day that fall when I asked him for a new prescription for methadone, he said, while pacing the floor with his tentative, careful steps: Let's stop for a few days. I'm afraid you may be taking too much of it. Later that day I felt very sick, which I had experienced a few times before. I was shaking and sweating and I had diarrhea. On top of that I was gripped by severe anxiety, which made my heart pound in panic. I knew I needed to have some of those pills, and I soon found a way to get them. For some reason I had kept one of Carl's old prescriptions, and I quickly copied it. I sent an unsuspecting Jabbe down to the pharmacy, and she came back with the pills, as if they were only a bottle of aspirin. After I had taken five or six of them – that's what I needed to have the same effect that two gave me at the start – I realized with a vague dismay that, for the first time in my life, I had done something criminal. I decided never to do that again. But I didn't hold to it. We lived in that house for five years, and, for most of the time, I was an addict.

4

If I hadn't gone to that dinner, my ear wouldn't have been operated on, and maybe from then on a lot of things would have been different. That was a period when Carl was only giving me shots once in a while. I stayed high on methadone, and the marks on my arms were getting fainter. My craving for Demerol was fading too. Whenever it reappeared, I reminded myself that I couldn't write under its influence, and I was completely preoccupied with working on my new novel. Life on Ewaldsbakken had taken on a nearly normal character. During the day I was with Jabbe and the children quite a bit, and in the evening, after we had eaten dinner, Carl and I went up to my room where we drank coffee, and Carl read his scientific books without saying much. A strange void stretched between us, and I realized that we were unable to hold a conversation. Carl had no interest in literature, and didn't seem to be interested in anything but his line of work. He sat with his pipe gripped between his uneven teeth, sticking out his lower jaw so it looked like it was supporting the rest of his face. At times he would raise his eyes from his book, smile to me shyly and say, So Tove, are you doing okay? He never told me about his childhood, as other men had, and if I asked about it, he gave me an empty, meaningless response, as if he couldn't remember anything about it. I often recalled Ebbe's evening ramblings, his recitations of Rilke poems in German and his dramatic Hørup passages. Lise, who made her way over to our place once in a while, told me that he was still grieving over losing me and that he was going to the Tokanten Pub and other places with Victor instead of doing his coursework.

Ester and Halfdan came by sometimes as well, when Carl wasn't home. They lived in an apartment on Matthæusgade. They had a little girl who was a year younger than Helle, and they were incredibly poor. They asked me why I had deserted all my old friends, and why I never came to the club anymore. I said that I was busy, and that it wasn't good for artists to socialize. Ester smiled sadly and said, Have you forgotten when we were at the Neckelhuset? But I was suffering from isolation and I longed for someone I could really talk to. I was a member of the Danish Authors' Association, but every time there was an event or a meeting, Viggo F. would call me to ask if I were going, because then he would stay away; so I never went. I was also a member of the exclusive PEN Club, whose director was Kai Friis Møller, one of my most effusive reviewers. He called me one day leading up to Christmas and asked if I would come to a dinner with him, Kjeld Abell, and Evelyn Waugh at Knights Restaurant. I said yes. I wanted to meet all three of them, and when Carl asked me, as usual, if I wouldn't rather have a shot, I said no to his tempting offer for the first time. That made him strangely ill at ease. If it gets too late, he said, I'll come and pick you up. But I said that I was sure I could get home on my own, and he could just go to bed. Well, he said quietly, make sure you cover up your arms. And put some cream on your face, he added, brushing my cheek with his finger. Your skin is still quite dry, and you might not realize it.

During the dinner I sat next to Evelyn Waugh, a small, vibrant, youthful man with a pale face and curious eyes. Friis Møller helped me gallantly over any language difficulties, and he was so attentive and kind in general that it was hard to believe he possessed such a sharp pen. Kjeld Abell asked Evelyn Waugh if they had such young and beautiful female authors in England. He said no, and when I asked what brought him to Denmark, he answered that he always took trips around the world when his children were home on vacation from boarding school, because he couldn't stand them. To excuse my conspicuous lack of appetite, I said that I'd had to eat with my kids before I left home. But I drank plenty, and I had also swallowed a handful of methadone pills before I left, so I was in a happy state and talked at length, making the two famous men laugh again and again. We were about the only guests in the restaurant. It was snowing outside, and it was so quiet that we could hear the thumping from ships' motors far out on the water. While we were enjoying our coffee and cognac, Friis Møller and Kjeld Abell suddenly stared in surprise at the exit, which I couldn't see, since I had my back to it. Who in the world is that? said Friis Møller, patting his mouth with his napkin. It looks like he's coming over here. I turned and saw, to my horror, Carl approaching in his high leather boots, his snow-covered leather jacket, his helmet in his hand, and that shy smile as if it were painted on his face. This . . . this is my husband, I said, confused, because he looked more like a Martian in the presence of these three elegant men, and it struck me that I had never really seen him in the company of others. He walked right over to me and said shyly, I think it's time for you to come home. Let me introduce myself, said Friis Møller, rising and pushing back his chair. Carl shook all their hands without saying a word, and an ironic smile appeared on Kjeld Abell's lips. I stood up, angry and miserable. My eyes were nearly blinded with embarrassment. In silence, Carl helped me put on my coat. When we were outside, I turned to him and said, What do you think you're doing? I said that you shouldn't come and get me. You embarrassed me. But it was impossible to fight with Carl. I wanted to go to bed, he said apologetically, but I couldn't without giving you your chloral. He opened the sidecar for me, and I sat on the seat while he closed the hatch again. During the ride home I cried over my humiliation. When he opened it up for me to get out, he saw my tears and exclaimed, What's the matter? Like in the old days I put my hand on my ear, because now I wanted to be truly comforted. Ow, I cried, this ear has been hurting me all evening. What do you think it could be? It looked like he was really worried. But there was also a faint glint of triumph in his eyes as he gave me a shot in one of the veins that was still open. I thought Falbe Hansen was wrong, he said. He went to bed with me, even more roughly than usual, and afterwards I lay limp and blissful, letting my fingers glide through his thin, reddish hair. He lay on his back with his hands under his head, staring up at the ceiling. We have to do something about this, he said. That bone has to be shaved down. But don't worry. I know an ear specialist who can't stand Falbe Hansen.

The next day he came home with all the fattest books the library had about ear illnesses. He studied them while we drank coffee, mumbling to himself, drawing red lines around the schematic drawings in them, feeling behind and around my ear, and saying that if I kept getting pain there, he would go to the doctor he suggested, and try to get him to do an operation. Is it hurting now? he asked. Yes, I said, making a face. It's hurting a lot. My craving for Demerol had returned with an uncontrollable force. The next day I wrote the last chapter of my novel, packed it in a neat cardboard cover, and wrote on it in capital letters: *For the Sake of the Child*, a novel by Tove Ditlevsen. Then I put it inside the locking cabinet in Carl's room, and I felt as I always did, a kind of mourning over not having the novel to occupy me anymore. I felt physically ill, and I took the bottle of pills from my locked desk drawer, which Carl couldn't open. I swallowed a handful without counting them. I had been very careful with my prescription writing. Sometimes I wrote Carl's name at the bottom and sometimes I wrote John's. He had gotten his degree from Avnstrup Sanatorium. Jabbe and I took turns having the prescriptions filled, and I'm convinced that the naive girl was never suspicious of me or of any of the secretive things that went on in that house. The syringe, the ampoules and the needles were locked inside the cabinet together with my papers, and only once – but that was much later – Jabbe said: That sure is a huge pharmacy bill, when she brought it to me. At that time it was several thousand kroner per month.

The specialist was old, surly and hard of hearing. When the female assistant didn't hand him the instruments he asked for immediately, he threw down whatever he was holding on the floor and yelled: Goddammit to hell, how am I supposed to work with such incompetent help? So, he said, looking in my ear, Falbe Hansen wouldn't operate? Well, we'll see about that. We'll take some X-rays. It could be it's reached the brain membrane. That's what I thought, Carl said. I think she's had a fever once in a while, too. Fever? I said, surprised. How high has it been? asked the doctor. We haven't taken it, said Carl calmly. I didn't want to worry my wife. But she often seems feverish and distracted. A few days later we were there again, and Carl and the doctor zealously studied the new X-rays. There's a shadow there, said the doctor, motionless, without saying anything more. Then he tossed his bald head and said, Fine, we'll operate. I can admit your wife tomorrow to a private room, and we can operate the same morning. When we got home I had a shot and thought, This is how I always want to live. I never want to return to reality again.

When I awoke from my anesthesia, my whole head was wrapped in gauze and then I finally learned what an earache was. I moaned in pain, rolling back and forth. The doctor came in and sat next to the bed. Try to smile, he said, and I formed my mouth into something resembling a smile. Why? I said, resuming my groaning and rolling. We touched the facial nerve, he explained, and that sometimes causes a paralysis, which we have luckily avoided. This hurts so much, I moaned. Can't you give me something for the pain? Of course, he said. You can have aspirin. That's the strongest medicine we give in this ward. We don't turn people into addicts. Aspirin and something to help you sleep at night. Would you call my husband? I said, horrified. I need to talk to him. He'll be here soon, said the doctor. In a little while. For now you need your rest. When Carl arrived he had his brown briefcase and inside it the blessed syringe. And when he gave me a shot in the open vein, I said, You have to come by all the time. I've never felt pain like this in my whole life, and here they only give you aspirin. They might as well give you sugar pills, he mumbled. You have to speak louder, I said. I can't hear you. You're deaf in that ear, he said. You will be for the rest of your life, but at least it won't hurt anymore. When the shot took effect, my pain receded into the background, but it was still there. What am I going to do, I asked sluggishly, when it comes back and you're not here? Try to stick it out, he said. They'll get suspicious if I come too often. He came back in the evening and gave me a shot and chloral. That was after several hours of hell, and I realized that I had never before known what real physical pain was like. I felt like I had been caught in a terrible trap, and where and when it would snap shut on me I couldn't predict. During the night I woke up. It felt as if flames were burning through my head. Help! I screamed out into the room, which was illuminated by the blue glow of the nightlight over the door. A nurse came running in. I'll give you a couple of aspirin, she said. I'm sorry we can't give you anything stronger. The doctor is so strict, she said apologetically. Both his ears were operated on, and he remembers how he endured the pain back then. After she left, I was gripped by wild panic. I couldn't stay there a minute longer. I got up and dressed, making as little noise as possible. Oh, oh, I moaned quietly to myself, I'm dying, Mother, I'm dying, I can't stand it. When I had put my coat on, I looked out carefully. Across from my room there was another door, which I hoped led to an exit. I ran across to it and soon found myself down on the deserted night street with my bandaged head. I waved for a taxi, and the driver asked me sympathetically if I had been in a car accident. When I got home, I ran up the garden walk and rang the bell like a madwoman. I didn't have my keys. Jabbe came and opened the door. What happened? she asked in alarm, staring at me wide-eyed. Nothing, I said. I just didn't want to be there anymore. I rushed into Carl's room and woke him up. Demerol, I moaned, quick. This pain is making me crazy.

It lasted for fourteen days. Carl stayed home from work

to give me shots whenever I asked for them. I lay motionless and limp in my bed and felt like I was being rocked to sleep in warm, green water. Nothing else in the world mattered to me but staying in this blissful state. Carl told me that lots of people are deaf in one ear, and that it doesn't really matter. I didn't care anyway, because it was worth it. No price was too high to be able to keep away intolerable real life. Jabbe came up and fed me. I almost couldn't get the food down and I pleaded with her to leave me in peace. No way, she said adamantly, not as long as I have any say in it. You're not going to starve to death. Things are bad enough as it is.

One night I woke up and realized that the pain was just about gone. But I was cold and shivering and I was so dehydrated that I had to use my fingers to pry apart my lips. Carl got up, drunk with sleep, and gave me a shot. I don't know what we're going to do, he said, when that vein clogs up too. Maybe we can find one in your foot.

While I was lying there alone in my bed, I realized that it had been a long time since I had seen my children. I walked down the stairs and into their room. I was so weak I had to lean against the wall to keep from falling. I turned on the light and looked at them. Helle was lying with her thumb in her mouth and her curls like a halo around her head. Michael was sleeping with his kitten in his arms; he couldn't sleep without it. And Trine was lying with her eyes open, watching me soberly with a child's inscrutable face. I fumbled my way to her bed and stroked her hair. She still had long blonde eyelashes, which she slowly lowered beneath my caresses. Toys were spread out all over the floor, and there was a playpen in the middle of the room. I almost didn't recognize these children anymore; I wasn't a part of their daily routine. Just like when an old woman thinks back on her youth, I thought how just a few years prior I was a happy and healthy young woman full of vitality and with lots of friends. But the thought was fleeting; I turned off the light and shut the door quietly behind me. It took me a long time to make it back upstairs to my bed. I left the light on, and I lay there, looking at my bony white hands, and I let my fingers move as if they were typing. Then I had a clear thought for the first time in a long while. If things get really bad, I thought, I'll call Geert Jørgensen and tell him everything. I wouldn't do it just for the sake of my children, but also for the sake of the books that I had yet to write.

5

Then time ceases to be relevant. An hour could be a year, and a year could be an hour. It all depends on how much is in the syringe. Sometimes it doesn't work at all, and I tell Carl, who is always nearby: There wasn't enough in it. He rubs his chin with a pained look in his eyes. We have to scale back, he says, otherwise you'll end up getting sick. I get sick if there's not enough in it, I say. Why do you let me suffer like this? Fine, fine, he mumbles, with a helpless shrug of his shoulders, I'll give you a little more.

I lie in bed continuously, and I need Jabbe's help to make it to the bathroom. When she sits down to feed me, her big face is all damp, as if someone spilled something on it. I brush her cheek with my finger and then stick it in my mouth. It tastes salty. Imagine that, I think enviously, to be able to feel sympathy for someone. I pay no attention to the seasons passing. The curtains are always closed, because the light hurts my eyes, so there's no difference between day and night. I sleep; I wake up; I'm sick or I'm well. I see my typewriter in the distance, as if I were looking backwards through binoculars. From the ground floor, where life is actually being lived, the children's voices reach me as through multiple layers of woolen blankets. Faces appear at my side and then vanish again. The telephone rings and Carl takes it. No, I'm sorry, he says, my wife isn't feeling well right now. He eats upstairs in my room, and I watch in wonder, and with a kind of distant envy, at his healthy appetite. Try to get a bite down, he says earnestly. It tastes really good. Jabbe made it just for you. He sticks a small piece of meat in my mouth with his fork, and I vomit it up again. I watch him wipe the spot off the sheet with a wet cloth. His face is close to mine. His skin is smooth and fine, and his eyelids are shiny and damp like a child's. You're so healthy, I say. You will be too, he says, if you could just bear to be a little sick for a while, if you would just let me cut back a little bit. Am I a real addict now? I ask. Yes, he says, with his shy, tentative smile, now you are a real addict. He tiptoes across the floor, pulls the curtain aside and looks at the weather. Won't it be nice, he says, when you can come down into the yard again? The fruit trees are in full bloom. How about having a look? He supports me while I stagger over to the window. Don't you cut the grass anymore? I ask, just to make conversation. Our grass is higher than our neighbor's. It's neglected and full of dandelions, whose tufts are blowing around in the wind. Well, he says, I have more important things to think about. One day he sits down next to me on the bed and asks if I'm feeling good. I am, because there was plenty in the last shot. He says, I have to talk to you about something. At the institute there's a specialist who took 40,000 kroner that he received for scientific studies and spent it on narcotics. I discovered it by chance. I say, I didn't know you even went there anymore. Well I do, he says, when you're sleeping, and he picks up some invisible fuzz from the floor – a new habit of his. So, I say, uninterested, so what do you have to do with that? I was thinking, he says, bending over again and picking up something, of going to a lawyer. At first I was going to go to the police, but don't you think it would be better to get advice from a lawyer first? I guess, I say, indifferently, that's probably better. But don't stay out too long. I need you here when I call you.

My mother comes by and sits by my bed. She takes my hand and pats it. Your father and I, she says, drying her eyes with the back of her hand, are of the opinion that Carl is making you sick. We can't say how exactly, but I don't think he's right in the head. He sounds so strange on the telephone, and he's never here when we come to visit. Jabbe says that he's become quite strange too. Recently he asked her to wash the soles of his shoes so they wouldn't carry germs. She says he frightens her. He's not making me sick, I say calmly. On the contrary, he's trying to make me well. Can you please leave? Talking makes me so tired. But once in a while I myself wonder if Carl's become a bit strange with his fuzz-picking, his tiptoeing and his locking himself in his room when I'm not calling for him. Once in a while I wonder, without any real fear, if I'm dying, and if I should pull myself together and call Geert Jørgensen. But if I do that, I won't get any more shots, that's for sure. If I do that, he'll admit me to the hospital, where they'll only give me aspirin. That's why I keep postponing, and I'm in a state where clear thoughts don't last for very long. Lise visits me and brings her face in close, and her cheek touches mine. I pull my face back with a start, because touching hurts. I can't bear the feel of other people's skin against mine, and it's been a long time since Carl went to bed with me. What's wrong with you, Tove? she asks soberly. You're hiding something, something terrible. Whenever anyone asks Carl, he answers with some nonsense. It's a blood illness, I say, because that's what Carl told me to say, but the worst is over. Now it's going to get better. Would you mind leaving? I'm so tired. Don't you ever write anymore? she says. Don't you remember, how you loved it when you were working on a book? Of course I do, I say, glancing at my dusty typewriter. I remember. It'll come back. Leave now.

Later I think about what she said. Will I ever write again? I remember that time long ago when sentences and lines of verse were always flying around my brain when the Demerol started working; but that doesn't happen anymore. That old blissfulness never comes back, and I know that Carl puts water in the syringe sometimes. One day or night while he's kneeling by my feet and sticking the syringe in a vein down there, I can see that his eyes are filled with tears. Why are you crying? I ask, surprised. I don't know, he says. But I want you to know that if I've done anything wrong I will be punished for it. That's the only confession he ever made. I think you're putting water in it, I say, because I don't care about anything else. Eventually you're going to feel pretty sick, he says, but afterwards you'll feel better, and in the end you'll be healthy again. But you have to stop pestering me, because I have never been able to bear to see you suffer. Everything I'm doing, I'm doing for you, for you to get better, so you can work again and be there for your children. His words fill me with terror. I will not live without Demerol, I shout at him. I can't live without it. You started this and you have to keep it up. No, he says quietly. I'm slowly cutting back.

Hell on earth. I'm freezing, I'm shaking, I'm sweating, I'm crying and yelling his name into the empty room. Jabbe comes in and sits by me. She is crying in despair. He's locked himself in his room, she says, and I'm afraid of him. I put his food outside his door and he takes it inside after I've gone.

Can't you call another doctor? You're so sick, and I can't do anything. When your friends come by, he tells me not to let them in. He won't even see his own mother. He might be going crazy, I say. I know that happened once before. Then I throw up, and Jabbe gets a bowl and dries my face with a washcloth. I ask her to find Geert Jørgensen's number in the telephone book and to write it down on a piece of paper. She does, and I put the note under my pillow. Now I'm unable to sleep, even with chloral. When I close my eyes I see horrible scenes on the insides of my eyelids. A little girl is walking down a dark street, and suddenly a man jumps out behind her. He has a black hood over his head, and he's carrying a long knife. He rushes at her and sticks the knife in her back. She screams, as I do too, and I open my eyes again. Carl comes tiptoeing in. Did you have another bad dream? he says, bending down, picking up fuzz from the floor. We're out of Demerol, he says. I must have forgotten to pay the last bill, but you can have an extra dose of chloral. He pours it into the measuring cup, and I plead with him to give me two. What the hell, he says, it won't hurt you, and he does what I ask. I feel a little bit better, and he pats my hand, which is only half as big as his. It's a question of nutrition, he says with a dopey grin. If you put on twenty pounds, things will be okay. He sits staring into space for a while. Then he starts to sing in a falsetto: We screw our women whenever we want to. That's from Regensen, he says. When I lived there I was a vegetarian. Sometimes I imagine that you're my sister, he mumbles, bending down to the floor again. Incest is more common than people think. Then he tries to go to bed with me, and for the first time I feel afraid of him. No, I say, pushing him away feebly. Leave me alone. I have to sleep. After he leaves, I'm immediately wide awake. He is crazy, I say to the empty air, and I'm dying. I try to focus on those two thoughts, which appear like two vertical strings inside my head, but they get pulled away like seaweed in stormy water. I don't dare close my eyes because of my visions. I wonder if it's night or day. I lift myself up on my elbow, and let myself slide out of bed. I realize that I don't have the strength to stand up. So I crawl on all fours across the floor and pull myself up onto my desk chair. It takes so much effort that I have to lay my head down on the typewriter keys and rest. My breathing wheezes in the silence. I have to take action before the chloral stops working. In my hand I'm clutching the note with Geert Jørgensen's telephone number. I turn on the desk lamp, dial the number, and wait for an answer. Hello, says a calm voice, this is Geert Jørgensen. I say my name. Oh, you! he says. This is quite a time to call and wake me up. Is something wrong? I'm sick, I say. He's putting water in the syringe. What syringe? Demerol, I say. I'm incapable of explaining anymore. Is he giving you Demerol? he says sharply. How long has this been going on? I don't know, I whisper. A few years, I guess, but now he doesn't want to do it anymore. I'm dying. Help me. He asks if I can come and see him the next day and I say no. Then he asks if he can speak to Carl, and I yell Carl's name as loud as I can, while I lay the phone down on the desk. He appears in the doorway in his striped pajamas. What is it? he asks sleepily. It's Geert Jørgensen, I say. He wants to talk to you. Oh, is that it, he says quietly, rubbing his unshaven chin. Then my career is ruined. He says it without reproach, and in that moment I don't know what he means. Hello, he says into the phone, and then he's quiet for a long time, because the other man is talking. I can hear all the way back in the room how agitated and angry he is. Carl just says, Right, tomorrow two o'clock. I'll be there. Yes, I'll explain it all tomorrow.

After he puts down the phone, he gives me a sick smile. Do you want a shot? he says gently. This time I'll put enough in; this calls for celebration. He gets the syringe, and the old blissfulness and sweetness from too long ago return to my blood. Are you angry with me? I say, twisting my fingers in his hair. No, he says, standing up. Everyone has to take care of themselves. Then he looks around the room, studying every single piece of furniture as if he were trying to imprint on himself the room and its furnishings. Do you remember, he says slowly, how happy we were the day we moved in? Yes, I say sluggishly, and we can be that way again. That was silly to call him. No, he says, that was your way out. You'll be admitted and everything will be over. What about the children? I say, remembering them. They have Jabbe, he says. She won't leave them. And what about you? I ask. What is your way out? I'm done, he says calmly. But don't you worry about that. We each have to salvage what we can.

The next day he comes home from Geert Jørgensen's and looks more relaxed than he has been in a long time. You have to be admitted, he says, taking off his motorcycle jacket, for drug rehab. It will start as soon as there's an empty spot at Oringe, and until then you can have all the Demerol you want. Isn't that good? Sure, I say, realizing that that was the same sentence that got me to succumb to the ear operation. And you, I ask, what are you going to do? I'm going to have some trouble with the healthcare authorities, he says with affected dismissiveness, but I'll take care of it. You have enough to deal with just thinking about yourself.

Jabbe is ecstatic when I tell her I'm going to be admitted. Then you're going to get all better, she says. All your friends and your family are going to be so happy. They've been so worried. The day I'm going to be admitted, she carries me down to the bathroom and washes me thoroughly. She washes my hair too, and the water gets filthy. When she carries me back up to bed she says, You don't weigh any more than Helle does. Carl comes in and gives me a shot. This is the last one, he says, but I'll ask them to go slow in there. I'll go with you.

I put my arm around the ambulance driver's neck while he carries me down the stairs. I think he looks worried, and I smile at him. He smiles back, and I see sympathy in his eyes. Carl sits down next to the stretcher, staring out into space. Suddenly he snickers as if he's just thought of something naughty. He picks up a couple of flecks of dust and rolls them between his hands. There's no guarantee, he says flatly, that we'll see each other again. Then he adds: Actually, I never was quite sure about that earache. That's the last sentence I ever hear him say.

6

I'm lying in bed with my head lifted slightly from the pillow, staring stiffly at my wristwatch. With the other hand I'm wiping the sweat out of my eyes. I'm staring at the second hand, because the minute hand won't move, and once in a while I hold the watch up to my good ear, because I think it's stopped. I get a shot every three hours, and the last hour is longer than all the years I have lived on this earth. It hurts my neck to hold up my head, but if I lay it down on the pillow, all the walls start moving in, closer and closer, so there's not enough air in my little room. If I lay my head down, all the creatures come scurrying across my blanket – small, disgusting, cockroach-like creatures by the thousands, crawling all over my body and getting inside my nose, my mouth and my ears. The same thing happens if I close my eyes for a moment. Then they're over me, and I can't stop them. I want to scream, but I can't get my lips apart. Besides, I have slowly been forced to admit that there's no use in screaming. No one is going to come before it's time. I am tied to the bed with a leather belt which cuts into my waist and makes it hard to turn. They don't even take it off when they change the sheets beneath me, which are always full of my excrement. 'They' are something blue and white, which flickers before my eyes with no identity. They're in control now, and it's no use calling out Carl's name endlessly until I get hoarse and my voice becomes an inaudible whisper. The time is five minutes to three. At three o'clock they will come and give me a shot. How can five minutes seem like five years? The watch ticks against my ear in rhythm to my frantic heartbeat. Maybe my clock is wrong, even though they constantly set it for me. Maybe they've forgotten me, maybe they're busy with other patients, whose screams and shouts reach me from the unknown world outside the door to my room.

Well, says a mouth, which to me seems to go from ear to ear in a face that is too large compared to its body, it's time for your shot. I get it in my thigh, and it takes some time before it starts to work. All it does is make me feel a little bit better. I'm able to put my head down on my pillow, and my body stops shaking like a leaf. The face in between the blue and white steps more distinctly closer. It is as pure and gentle as the face of a nun, and I understand that this person does not wish me harm. Talk to me, I ask, and she sits down next to me and wipes the sweat from my face. She says, This will all be over soon. We'll get you back on your feet, but you certainly did get here at the last moment. I ask, Where's my husband? Dr Borberg will come in to speak with you shortly, she says, evading my question. First we have to get you cleaned up a bit. Then I'm lifted up by strong hands while the sheet below me is changed. I'm washed, and then dressed in a clean, white shirt. The worst thing, I say, is all the creatures. I'll get rid of them, she says. Just call me when they come, and I'll chase them away. Now look here. Be a really good girl and drink all of this I have here for you. You're badly dehydrated. Can't you tell? Aren't you thirsty? She lifts my head and puts a glass to my lips. Now drink, she says earnestly. I drink as she asks and I even ask for more. That was good, says the voice. You are a real sweetheart.

Then Dr Borberg comes in, the only human in this world of misery that I perceive clearly. He is a tall blond man in his mid-thirties with a round, boyish face and intelligent, friendly eyes. He asks if I'm able to speak with him for a moment. Then he says, Your husband has been admitted to the National Hospital. He's suffering from a serious psychosis. The Department of Health has brought a case against him, but now it's possible that they will drop it. What about the children, I say, horrified. Jabbe has no money when he's not there. I have to go straight home. You won't be going home for six months, the doctor says firmly, but of course your young housekeeper will need money. I have spoken to her on the telephone, and she will come to see you one day soon. I'll make sure that you're able to talk with her right after you've had your injection. He leaves, and the shot slowly wears off. Then I lie there again, my head lifted off the pillow, staring at my watch, and there is nothing else in the world but it and me.

When Jabbe came, I gave her the bank book, which Carl had placed on the stretcher in the ambulance. Then I asked her to get the manuscript of my novel from the cabinet in Carl's room, and give it to the publisher. I also asked her to stay with the children until I came back home, and she promised she would. She sat observing me with her damp, devoted eyes, patting my hand and asking if I was getting anything to eat. Then she started telling me lots of things about the children, but I couldn't pay attention. Please leave now, Jabbe, I said, while sweat poured out from my whole body. Tell the children I'll be better soon and that I'm looking forward to seeing them so much. Your husband, she said with an anxious look, he's not going to suddenly come back home again, is he? No, I told her, I don't think he will ever be coming back home.

Gradually my miseries lessened. Now I was able to put my head down on my pillow without the walls creeping in around my bed, and I stopped staring at my watch constantly. I was let out of the belt, and I was allowed to go to the toilet supported by one of the nurses. Outside my room, there was a larger room where the beds were so close together that there was only a narrow walkway between them. Most of the patients had belts on, and some of them had large mittens on their hands. They stared at me with empty, glassy eyes, and I pulled closer to the nurse. Don't be afraid, she said. These are just people who are very sick. They won't hurt anyone. But they were yelling and screaming so loud that you couldn't hear your own voice. Why am I here? I asked. I'm not mentally ill. This is a locked ward, she said. You couldn't be anywhere else when you first arrived. When you get better, I'm sure you'll be moved to an open ward. Come here, she said gently, leading me to a sink. Wash your hands. See if you can do it yourself. When I raise my head, I see myself in the mirror, and I put my hand over my mouth to hold back a scream. That's not me, I cry, I don't look like that. That's not possible. In the mirror I see a worn-out, aged, stranger's face with gray, scaly skin and red eyes. I look like I'm seventy, I sob, clinging to the nurse, who leans her head in on my shoulder. There, there, she says. I didn't think of that, but don't cry. When you start getting insulin it will be much better. You'll get more meat on your bones and you'll look like a young woman again. I promise. It happens all the time. When I'm in bed again, I lie there looking at my toothpick arms and legs, and for a moment I'm full of rage at Carl. Then I remember that I carry my share of the blame as well, and my rage disappears.

Early the next morning I got a shot of insulin. I had slept poorly that night, and I dozed off again until I woke at nine-thirty. I felt ravenously hungry. I was shaking, and black dots flickered before my eyes. My whole organism was screaming for food like before it had screamed for Demerol, and I rushed out into the corridor and called for a nurse. Mrs Ludvigsen was her name. I feel sick, I said. Can I have some food? She took me by the arm and led me back to my room. Actually, she said, you don't get your meal until ten o'clock, but I'll bring it to you now. That will be okay just this once. When she came in with the tray, which had on it a plate piled with rye bread with cheese and wheat bread with jelly, I grabbed the food before she even had a chance to put down the tray, and I shoved the food in my mouth, and chewed and swallowed and grabbed for more, while a previously unknown sense of physical well-being spread through my body. Wow, I feel great, I blurted out between two slurps of milk. Can I have all the food I can eat? Mrs Ludvigsen laughed. Yes, she said, even if you eat us out of house and home. It's wonderful to see you eating. She brought more food and I ate like crazy, laughing with bliss. I am so happy, I said. I think I'm finally going to be healthy again. You won't take the insulin away from me again will you? Not before you have reached your normal weight, she said. Later I put on a hospital gown and I sat in a chair by the window. Outside was a large, manicured lawn, and between two low buildings I could see a strip of blue water with white foam. It was fall, and the withered leaves were collected in neat piles on the grass. Some men in striped clothing were raking them, without much enthusiasm. When can I go for a walk? I asked Mrs Ludvigsen while she was brushing my hair. Soon, she promised. One of us will go with you. You're not allowed to go alone yet.

A period followed when I looked at my watch to see if it was time to eat soon. I looked forward to meals, and I ate like a bricklayer. I gained weight, and they weighed me every other day. When I was admitted, I weighed thirty kilos, but now I was up to forty. I could walk without help, and every day I went outside and talked non-stop with the nurse about everything under the sun, because I was in a terrific mood. I realized I felt like I did back in that happy time before I had met Carl. I was allowed to call home every day, and I even spoke on the phone with Helle. She was now six years old and going to school. She said, Mommy, why don't you get married to Daddy again? I don't like daddy Carl. I laughed and said that I might, but that I didn't know if he would want me back. He's not drinking anymore, she said hopefully. He's going to school instead. He was here yesterday with Victor. Victor gave us candy and caramel creams. He was so nice. He asked if I was going to be a writer like my mother.

One afternoon, right after I had eaten, Dr Borberg came to see me. We need to have a serious conversation, he said as he sat down. I sat on the edge of the bed, looking at him expectantly. I'm healthy again, I said. I'm so happy. Then he explained to me that I was regaining my physical health, but that there was much more to it. There would be a stabilizing process, and that was what would take the longest time. I was going to have to learn how to live a bare, unaffected life, and every memory of Demerol would slowly disappear from my mind. It's easy, he said, to feel healthy and happy in this protected hospital room. But when you get home and experience adversity – like we all do – the temptation will return. I don't know, he said, when your husband will be completely well, or even if he ever was, but you must never see him again, no matter what happens, and we will make sure that he never visits you. The doctor asked me if I had ever gone to other doctors, and I told him no. He also asked if Carl had ever given me anything other than Demerol, and I told him methadone. That is just as dangerous, he said. You must never have that again either. Then I told him that I would keep away from it for the rest of my life, because I would never forget all the horrible suffering I'd been through. Yes, you will, he said soberly. You will forget it all soon enough. If you are ever tempted by something like that, you'll think, what harm could it do? You'll think that you can control it, and before you know it, you'll be caught again. I laughed carelessly, You don't think very much of me, do you? We have had very sad experiences with addicts, he said. Only one out of a hundred ever fully recover. Then he smiled and patted me kindly on the shoulder. But sometimes, he said, I think that you are that one, because your case is so unusual, and because, in contrast to so many others we see, you have something to live for. Before he left, he gave me grounds permission, which meant that I could walk outside on the property for one hour every day

Time passed, and I felt at home in the ward and on the beautiful grounds, where now and again I had a nice chat with one of the other patients who was out walking. I felt so attached to the personnel, that I declined the offer to move to a better ward. Jabbe brought me my typewriter and my clothes, which were in sad shape, since I hadn't bought anything new for years. She also made sure that I had some money, and one day I got permission to travel alone to Vordingborg to buy myself a winter coat. All I had was my old trench coat back from my time with Ebbe, and it wasn't warm. I left for the town late in the afternoon. Twilight was approaching, and a few pale stars emerged in the sky, bleached by the city lights. My mind was relaxed and carefree, and my thoughts kept returning to my time with Ebbe. I thought about what Helle said: Mommy, why don't you get married to Daddy again? I had begun letters to him numerous times, but they always ended up in the trash. I had caused him so much unnecessary misery, and he would never be able to understand why.

After I had bought my coat and put it on, I walked back down the main street without stopping to look in the shop windows. I was hungry and looking forward to dinner. Then my attention was suddenly caught by a well-lit pharmacy window. It radiated a muted light from containers of mercury and beakers filled with crystals. I kept standing there, while the yearning for small white pills, which were so easy to get, rose inside me like a dark liquid. Horrified, I realized while I stood there that the longing was inside me like rot in a tree, or like an embryo growing all on its own, even though you want nothing to do with it. I pulled myself away reluctantly, and kept walking. The wind blew my long hair over my face, and I pushed it aside angrily. I thought about Dr Borberg's words: If you are ever tempted . . .

When I got back I took out a piece of typing paper and looked at it. It would be so easy to cut it with scissors, write a prescription for methadone and walk into the pharmacy and have it filled. Then I thought about how much they had done for me here, and how genuinely people shared my joy over being healthy again, and I felt I couldn't just let them down like that. Not as long as I was here. I walked out to the bathroom, gathered up my courage, and looked in the mirror. I hadn't done that since the day when I had been so horrified by my appearance. I smiled happily to myself and touched my round, smooth cheeks. My eyes were clear and my hair was shiny. I didn't look one day older than I was. But when I went to bed and had been given my chloral, I lay awake for a long time, thinking about that pharmacy window. I thought how well I had worked on methadone; all I had to do was not increase the dosage. Then I remembered the endless suffering during my rehab and thought: no, never again. The next day I wrote to Ebbe and asked if he would come and visit me. A few days later I got his answer. He wrote that if I had called for him a few months prior, he would have come right away. But now he had met another woman, and everything was starting to go better for him. You can't expect, he wrote, to abandon a person for five years and then find him in the same place when you return.

I cried when I read his letter. No man had ever turned me down before. Then I thought about the house on Ewaldsbakken, the neglected yard and my three children, who didn't know their mother anymore, just as I didn't think I knew them. I was going home to be alone with them and Jabbe, and it felt like I wasn't suited for it. For the rest of the time I was at Oringe I never went into town again, so I wouldn't see that pharmacy window.

7

It's springtime when I return to the house on Ewaldsbakken. The gardens are scenting the air with forsythia and golden rain, which drape over our hedge by the narrow gravel road. Jabbe has put out chocolates and a homemade pastry, and the children are all sitting clean and finely dressed around the festive table. At the center of the table, a cardboard sign is leaning against a vase with flowers. Welcome Home Mommy it reads, in crooked capital letters. Helle says she made it herself. She looks at me with her crooked Ebbe-eyes, awaiting my praise. The two little ones are shy and quiet, and when I try to stroke the head of Trine, our little outsider, she pushes away my hand and reproachfully leans in toward Jabbe. I think how it was Jabbe who guided their first steps, Jabbe who talked gibberish with them, blew on their scrapes, and sang them to sleep in the evening. Only Helle shows me any closeness, talking to me as if I'd never been away. She tells me that her daddy has gotten married to a woman who writes poems just like I do. But you are much prettier, she says loyally, and Jabbe laughs as she pours me something to drink. Your mother, says Jabbe, is just as pretty as the day

I first saw her. When the children are in bed later, I sit up chatting with Jabbe. She has bought a bottle of blackcurrant brandy, which we share, while an indefinable longing inside me diminishes slightly. It's better to drink a little once in a while, says Jabbe, whose cheeks are pink and whose eyes are shinier than usual, than all that crap your husband put in you. So, I say, now you want to make me an alcoholic? I'm going straight from the frying pan into the fire! We both laugh, and we agree that she'll have every Wednesday afternoon and every other weekend off. The poor girl hasn't had a vacation in years. She asks me what she's going to do with herself, and I suggest that she put a personal ad in the newspaper. I want to do the same thing. People aren't meant to be alone, I say. I get a piece of paper and a pencil, and we have a lot of fun creating two ads, where we describe ourselves as having every attribute that a man could want. We get rather silly, and it's late before I go up to bed. Jabbe has decorated my room with fresh flowers, but the memories of everything that happened to me here overwhelm me suddenly, and I lie down on the bed fully dressed. I think I can see the shadow of a figure walking around, picking up bits of dust while mumbling to himself. I wonder, where is he now? I walk over to the window, open it, and lean out. There is a clear, starry sky. The handle of the Big Dipper is pointing right at me, and out on the poorly lit road a couple are embracing. They kiss one another under a streetlamp. Quickly I shut the window, realizing I feel like I used to when I was married to Viggo F., when the entire world was filled with loving couples. With a heavy heart I undress and go to bed. Then I realize I forgot to get milk for my chloral. I got a bottle of it from the hospital, and Dr Borberg says that he will send me a prescription for more when this one is used up. He doesn't want me to go to any other doctors. When he said goodbye, he told me to call him if I had any problems, or just so he could know how I was doing. I get milk from the kitchen and go back to bed. I pour myself three doses instead of the two I usually get, and while the deadening effect spreads inside me, I think how it's springtime, and I'm still young, and there's no man in love with me. I embrace myself involuntarily, curl up my pillow, and pull it close as if it were alive.

The days pass steadily and evenly, and I'm always with Jabbe and the children. Being alone in my room makes me sad, and I have no desire to write. The kids get used to me, and now they run to me just as often as they run to Jabbe. Jabbe tells me that I should go out and meet people. She wants me to visit my family and my friends again, but something is holding me back. Maybe it's my old fear that someone will find out what was happening at my house. One morning I wake up particularly depressed. I hear rain falling outside, and my room is filled with a gray, dreary light. The pharmacy window in Vordingborg appears with a clarity in my mind's eye as if I hadn't seen it only once, but a hundred times. I see the pile of paper on my desk. Just two, I think, two every morning, never more than that. What harm could it do? I get out of bed, shuddering with discomfort. Then I sit down at my desk, take out a pair of scissors, and cut out a rectangular-shaped piece of paper. I write it out carefully, get dressed, and tell Jabbe that I'm going for a morning walk. I signed Carl's name, and I'm sure that, wherever he is in the world, he'll cover for me, if it comes to that. When I get back, I take two pills and stand there looking at the bottle. I have allotted myself two hundred. I remember my suffering in rehab, and faintly I hear Borberg's voice inside of me: You will soon forget. Suddenly I become frightened at myself, and I lock the pills inside the cabinet. I slide the key far under my mattress without really knowing why. When the pills take effect, I'm filled with bliss and initiative, and I sit down at my typewriter and write the first couplet of a poem which I have thought about working on for a long time. The first couplet always comes easy. When I'm done and I think the poem is good, I feel a strong urge to talk to Dr Borberg. I call him on the phone and he asks me how things are going. Good, I say. The sky is blue and the grass is greener than usual. There is a pause on the other end. Then he says sharply, Listen, what have you taken? Nothing, I lie, I just feel good. Why do you ask? Forget it, he says with a laugh, it's just my suspicious nature.

I go down to the kitchen and help Jabbe peel potatoes while the children swirl around us. It's Sunday, so Helle is home from school. We have coffee at the kitchen table, and afterwards I go with the children into the nursery, where I read aloud for them from *Grimms' Fairy Tales*. After lunch I feel so depressed and preoccupied that Jabbe asks me worriedly, Is something the matter? No, I say, I just need a nap. I go up and lie down, staring at the ceiling with my hands under my head. Two more, I think. That couldn't do any harm, compared with how many I used to throw down in the old days. When I go into Carl's room, I see that the key is not in the cabinet. Where in the world could I have put it? I have no idea, and suddenly I'm gripped with panic. An anxious sweat breaks out under my arms, and I turn the room upside down. I'm looking frantically and I realize that it's Sunday. I'm pretty sure the pharmacy is closed. I empty all the desk drawers onto the table, turning them over, knocking their bottoms; but the key isn't there. I need those pills, just two more, and I can't think any further than that. I go downstairs. Jabbe, I say, something terrible has happened. The key to the cabinet is lost, and I have some papers in there that I need right away. It can't wait until tomorrow. Practical Jabbe says that we can just call a locksmith. She did that once when she was locked out of the house. They work around the clock, she says, and she looks in the telephone book and finds me the number. I run upstairs to the telephone and explain to the man that a key to a desk has been lost. Inside the desk there's some vital medicine that I need right away. Then he comes over and picks the lock. There you are, ma'am. Your sorrows are over. That will be twenty-five kroner. After he leaves, I take four pills and think, with the clear, observing part of my consciousness, that now I'm caught again, and that it'll take a miracle to stop me. But the next day I take just two in the morning, like I had originally decided. And when the temptation to take more strikes, it seems to be enough to just hold the bottle in my hand. There it is and it's not going anywhere. It's mine and no one can take it away from me.

A few nights later I'm awoken by the telephone. Hi, says a cottony voice, this is Arne. Sinne is in London, and when she comes back we're getting divorced. But that's not why I called. Victor and I are here at my house having a drink, and we want to come and visit you. It's crazy that you and Victor have never met. Can we come over? No, I say, irritated. I'm sleeping. He continues, Then how about tomorrow, in broad daylight? To get rid of him, I say okay. When I'm back in bed, after having pulled the phone plug out, I remember that tomorrow is Jabbe's day off. Hopefully they won't call back. In the morning I've forgotten all about it. I take my two pills and go down and eat breakfast with Jabbe and the children. After Jabbe leaves, the phone rings again. It's Arne and he's even more drunk than he was the night before. We're sitting here in Green's having a quiet beer, he says. We'll be over in half an hour. After I hung up, I went upstairs and took four pills to help me get through this. Then I dressed the little ones and went for a walk with them down the street. It was July and I was wearing a blue summer dress I had bought one day when I was out with Jabbe. On the way home, a taxi passed us, and in the rear window I saw Arne's drunk, round face next to someone else whom I couldn't make out. The car made it to the house before us, and the two men stepped out, their arms full of bottles. Hi, Tove, shouted Arne. Here I am with Victor. I greeted them, and the man named Victor kissed my hand. He seemed pretty sober, and the sight of him made all my irritation disappear. I let go of the children's hands, and they ran into the house. I couldn't see Victor's eyes because of the sun, but his mouth had the most beautiful cupid's bow shape that I had ever seen. His entire person radiated a kind of disheveled demonic vitality that absolutely fascinated me. I brought them inside, and Arne immediately passed out on Carl's bed. I asked Helle to take care of the little ones for a while, and I took Victor up to my room. He sat down and looked at me without saying anything. I sat in another chair, and my heart was pounding. I was filled with a mixture of happiness and panic at the same time. Panic like when I was a child and my mother was sobbing: I'm leaving; and my brother and I didn't know what would become of us. Victor knelt down in front of me and started caressing my ankles. I love you, he said. I love your poems. For years I've wanted to meet you. I turned his face up toward mine, and I said, Until now I always thought all that talk about love at first sight was a lie. I took his head in my hands and kissed his beautiful lips. Below his tired eyes there were deep smoke-colored shadows, and two wrinkles ran down his cheeks as if they were tracks made by tears. He had a face full of suffering and passion. Don't leave me, I said intently. Don't ever leave me again. It was strange saying that to someone I had just met for the first time, but Victor didn't seem at all surprised by it. No, he said, pulling me close. No, I will never leave you again. Then we went downstairs to the children, who knew Victor from previous visits, while I was at Oringe. Look here, Helle, he said. Here's ten kroner. Now run off and buy red candies for all three of you. After we ate, Helle looked enchantedly at Victor and said, Mommy, can't you marry him so we can have a daddy in the house again? Victor laughed and said, I'll think about it.

I'm head over heels in love with you, I said, when we were lying back in my bed. Will you stay overnight? I will, for the rest of my life, he said, smiling with his blindingly white teeth. What about your wife? I asked. We have the law of love on our side, he said. That law, I said, kissing him, gives us the right to hurt other people. We made love and talked for most of the night. He told me about his childhood, and it was a lot like Ebbe's childhood, but it was still as if I were hearing it for the first time. I told him about the five years of craziness with Carl and about my time at Oringe. I didn't know a person could get so sick from being an addict, he said, surprised. I just thought it was like when the rest of us drink beer. That it's just something you need to be able to cope with life. Eventually he fell asleep, and I lay there observing his face with its elegant nostrils and exquisite mouth. I remembered the time I said to Jabbe: Imagine having feelings for someone. Now I could, and it was the first time since I had met Ebbe. I wasn't alone anymore, and I felt like it wasn't just drunken babble when he said he would stay with me for the rest of our lives. I took my chloral and snuggled close to him. His blond hair had the scent of a child's who had just come home after playing in the grass and sunshine.

8

From then on, Victor and I were almost always together. He only went home when he needed his wife to wash and iron a shirt for him, and I laughed and said that in years to come I might be fulfilling that role. Victor had a four-year-old daughter whom he adored, and he often talked about her. He played hooky from work every other day, and when he did show up, he and I talked on the phone every hour. He was an economics major, just like Ebbe, and he was also more interested in literature, just like Ebbe. Victor would pace back and forth in my room, pretending to be Prince Andrei from Tolstoy's *War and Peace* or d'Artagnan from *The Three Musketeers*. He would fence with an invisible sword and act out huge battle scenes where he played all the roles himself. His lean figure would move around the room while quotations flowed from his lips until he collapsed, exhausted and laughing, onto the bed. I was born at the wrong time, he said – a couple of centuries too late. But if I were born then, I would never have met you. He took me in his arms and we forgot everything in the world around us. Our passion was barely satisfied before it was aroused again, and the children were once more left in

Jabbe's care. That's the terrible thing about love, I said, that you lose interest in other people. That's right, he said, and then it always hurts so damned much in the end. One day he came over happily and told me that his wife had asked for a divorce. So he moved in with me, taking nothing with him but his clothes and his books. He didn't care about material things. About the same time I got a call from a lawyer who had been asked by Carl to arrange our divorce. He explained that Carl wanted the house sold so he could get half its value. Then we'll sell it, said Victor. We can find somewhere else to live.

But a shadow was falling across our happy days, though Victor hadn't noticed it yet. I was taking more and more methadone for fear that I would get sick if I didn't. I lost my appetite and lost weight, and Victor said that I looked like a gazelle who had decided to be eaten by a lion. I took the pills arbitrarily and never really knew how many I needed. Once in a while I wanted to call Dr Borberg and tell him all about it. I was tempted to tell Victor too, but I resisted, for fear that I would lose him.

Early one Sunday morning we rode our bicycles out to Dyrehaven to have coffee in a little out-of-the-way café where we had become regulars. I had taken four methadone before we left, but I forgot to take the bottle with me. We sat there, staring into one another's eyes, and the waiter smiled at us forbearingly. Who knows what he's thinking, I said. Victor laughed. I'm sure you know, he said, that nothing looks as foolish as other people in love. He just thinks we're amusing. Victor placed his hand over mine. You look like an odalisque, he said, and he had to explain to me what an odalisque was. The sky was unbroken blue, and the birdsong had a particular spring joy to it. On the red checkered tablecloth a goldfinch sat eating crumbs, and the moment was planted in my memory like something I could always take out and experience again, no matter what might happen. We took a walk in the woods holding hands, and I told Victor about my marriage to Viggo F., and about how back then I couldn't bear seeing young couples in love. The time flew by and Victor suggested we go back to the restaurant and eat lunch. Suddenly I felt a cold shiver run through me, as if I was being attacked from behind, and I knew what that meant. I dropped Victor's hand. No, I said, I'd rather go home. No, let's not, he said, surprised, and slightly uncomfortable. We're having such a great time; there's no need to rush home. I stood still and put my arms around myself to try and keep warm. My mouth started watering and I felt like I was about to throw up. I blurted out: You know what, I have some pills at home that I really need to get. I can't stay here without them. Can't we go home? Worried, he asked me what kind of pills they were, and I said that the name wouldn't mean anything to him. Then you're still an addict, he said uneasily. I thought that having me would be enough. As we rode home, I told him that I was going to slowly cut back, because I wanted to quit. He was enough for me, it was just a physical dependency that made me need the pills. I also told him, while I was quickly pedaling, that I would call Dr Borberg and ask what to do. Do that as soon as we get home, he said, with an authority that I had never heard from him before. We got home and I took four pills. Then I called Dr Borberg. I'm in love, I said. We're living together and his name is Victor. I certainly hope he's not a doctor, said Borberg. Then I told him about the fake prescriptions and that I wanted to quit, but that I couldn't do it by myself. He was quiet a moment. Then he said flatly, Let me talk to Victor. I gave Victor the phone, and Borberg talked to him for about an hour. He explained to Victor what addiction meant, and what he would have to contend with if he loved me. When Victor put down the phone, he was a changed person. His face radiated a cold, hard will, and he put out his hand towards me. Give me those pills, he said. Scared, I ran and got them and he put them in his pocket. You get two each day, he said, no more, no less. And when there's no more left, that's it. No more fake prescriptions. If I find out that you write even one more, I won't have anything to do with you ever again. Don't you love me anymore? I asked, sobbing. Yes, I do, he said. That's why.

The following days I was miserable. Then it passed and we were both happy again. Now it's over once and for all, I promised Victor. You mean more to me than all the pills in the world. We sold the house and moved into a four-room apartment in Frederiksberg with Jabbe and all the children.

In the middle of fall, Helle was sick one night. She came into our room and crawled up in bed with us, shivering with fever. She had a sore throat, and I took her temperature, which was over 40°C. I asked Victor what we should do, and he said he would phone the night doctor on call. Half an hour later the doctor arrived. He was a tall, friendly man who looked down Helle's throat and wrote a prescription for penicillin. Children get fevers more easily than adults, he said. But just to be safe I'll give her a shot right now. When he opened his bag, I saw syringes and ampoules, and my craving for Demerol, which I thought had been buried far away, returned and uncontrollably consumed my entire consciousness. Victor always fell asleep before I did, and he was a heavy sleeper. The following night I crept out of bed and carefully lifted the phone receiver in the living room. I dialed the doctor on call and then sat down on a stool with my legs tucked under me while I waited. I left the door open so he wouldn't ring the bell. I was half terrified that Victor would find me out, but what compelled me was stronger than my fear. When the doctor arrived, I said I had an earache that was killing me. He looked in the ear that had been operated on and asked me, Can you take morphine? No, I said, it makes me throw up. Then we'll try something else, he said, and he filled a syringe. I prayed to heaven it was Demerol. It was, and I got back into bed next to my sleeping Victor, while the old bliss and sweetness flowed through my whole body. Happily oblivious, I thought I could do this as often as I wanted. There wasn't much risk involved.

But a few nights later, while the night doctor on call was pulling out the syringe, Victor suddenly walked into the living room. What the hell is going on here? he yelled angrily at the frightened doctor. There's nothing wrong with her! Get out of here this instant and don't ever set foot in this house again! After the doctor left, Victor gripped my shoulders so firmly that it hurt. You damned little devil, he snarled. If you ever do that again, I'm leaving you.

But he didn't. He never did. He fought against his terrible rival with a constant vigor and rage that filled me with horror. Whenever he was tempted to give up the fight, he would call Dr Borberg, whose words gave him renewed strength. I had to abandon the night doctors, because Victor hardly dared to sleep anymore. But when he was at work, I visited other doctors and got them to give me shots without much difficulty. To protect myself, I would tell Victor about it in the evening. He called up lots of doctors and threatened to report them to the Department of Health, so I wouldn't be able to go back to them anymore. But in my wild hunger for Demerol I always found new ones. I hardly ate. I lost weight again, and Jabbe was seriously worried about my health. Dr Borberg told Victor that if I kept this up, I would have to be readmitted, but I begged him to let me stay home. I promised I would change and then I broke my promises. Finally Dr Borberg told Victor that the only real solution would be for us to move away from Copenhagen. At the time we didn't have much money, but we got a loan from Hasselbalch Publishing and bought a house in the suburb of Birkerød. There were five doctors in the town, and Victor visited every one of them right away and forbade them to have anything to do with me. So it was impossible for me to get the drug, and slowly I adapted to accept life as it was. Victor and I loved each other, and having one another and the children was enough for us. I started writing again, and whenever reality got under my skin, I bought a bottle of red wine and shared it with Victor. I was rescued from my years of addiction, but ever since, the shadow of the old longing still returns faintly if I have to have a blood test, or if I pass a pharmacy window. It will never disappear completely for as long as I live.